Juliet Cattle-Burke was born in Plymouth, at the tail end of the 1960s, to June and David. She has an older sister and two younger brothers.

Juliet has worked as a teaching assistant in the same school for over twenty-six years.

This book is dedicated to the memory of my mother,
who I miss every single day.

Juliet Cattle-Burke

GINTON ABBEY:

VOLUME TWO

To Becky,

Enjoy even more debauchery!

love @ Jule oxi

AUSTIN MACAULEY PUBLISHERS™

LONDON · CAMBRIDGE · NEW YORK · SHARJAH

A CIP catalogue record for this title is available from the British Library.

ISBN 9781398407169 (Paperback)
ISBN 9781398415805 (ePub e-book)

www.austinmacauley.com

First Published 2022
Austin Macauley Publishers Ltd®
1 Canada Square
Canary Wharf
London
E14 5AA

I would like to say thank you to my friend, Sharon Stacey, who set up a Facebook page to help spread the word (most of them rude, filthy and obscene!) of Ginton Abbey.

Thanks to friends and fans, old and new, who help pass on the filth to others!

Last but not least, thank you to my husband who is always there for me. I love you…MORE!

Chapter One

Phokker was pounding away. BANG! BANG! BANG! Until his hand was sore.

"Time to get up, Jack!" he bellowed through the door.

Jack started to rouse and stretched himself out broadly. "What time is it?" asked Jack, "It's still bleeding dark!"

"It's half past five and there's work to be done!" shouted Phokker.

"Work at half past five?" squeaked Jack, "What the bloody hell goes on at half past five?"

"LOTS!" yelled Phokker, "Now get up, get dressed and meet me in the kitchen!"

Jack was very surprised at the tone which Phokker used. He was so nice yesterday, so what the hell happened? Phokker, as you may well recall, had been calling out Molly's name and had sleepwalked, and Jack returned him to his bed. Phokker felt very irritable this morning as he had dreamt about Molly, but he had no knowledge of calling out her name or the sleepwalking. He hated the way he felt after dreaming about her and needed to get her out of his head. "Morning, Mrs Spanner; morning, Kitty," he called out as he stepped into the kitchen. There was silence there – surely these two weren't still in bed? They rise earlier than he does!

"Hello. Is anyone there?" he called out.

He could see that the range was lit and the copper kettle was close to boiling point. The table was set for breakfast, but there was no sign of the women. He removed the kettle from the range and set it aside. He looked in the courtyard but found no one. He checked in the wash house; empty. He wandered around the back to look into the garden to see if they were chatting to Dickens, but all he found was Dickens' chickens scratching about. "Where the hell are they?" he said out loud and stormed back towards the kitchen. This was going to be a really shitty day for him. He slammed the kitchen door and shouted up the back stairs for Jack. It echoed and shook the tiny panes of glass in the small staircase windows.

"APPY BURFDAY!" came a chorus from behind him.

"WHAT THE FUCK?" Phokker yelled, completely startled, and held himself up by the door frame, clutching his chest. There, stood by the cellar door were Mrs Spanner, Kitty, Jack and Dickens with huge grins on their faces. Mrs Spanner walked towards the kitchen table with a massive Victoria sponge cake.

"Appy burfday, Phokker," she smiled at him. Phokker composed himself from his near-crumpled heap and straightened his tie. Kitty came and gave him a big squeeze.

"I did 'ave somethin' for yer burfday," she said, "but now I got Jack. Queenie says I'm not allowed to give that away anymore."

Phokker smiled.

"Well bugger me," said Mrs Spanner, "I wondered when Phokker was goin' to show up!"

"I'm sorry everyone," he said, "I was a little taken aback."

"Come and 'ave yer breakfast," said Mrs Spanner. She popped the kettle back onto the range and started to cook the eggs and bacon.

"How old are you?" asked Jack.

"50," replied Mrs Spanner.

"How did you know that?" Phokker asked her.

"You'd not long had your 40th when you came 'ere. You been 'ere ten years so…"

"That makes me 50; rightly so," interrupted Phokker.

"I ain't as green as I'm cabbage looking, you know!" she said.

"No one thinks that of you, Mrs Spanner," Phokker replied.

"Them up there do," she said, pointing upwards to indicate His Lord and Ladyship.

"They don't matter, Queenie," said Kitty,

"We're your real friends." Mrs Spanner smiled.

"Well bugger me!" said Kitty, "There you are!" and everyone laughed.

Jack looked at Dickens' roaring gob. "Didn't you have three teeth yesterday?" he asked him.

"Mmmph crumple pherr mmim weasel mmph fell 'nip," replied Dickens, gesturing wildly.

"Oh, I see," said Jack, "but didn't that hurt?"

"Phiss imm werzz themmunchin not 'urt," said Dickens, manically waving.

"Let's hope that don't happen again!" said Jack, and Dickens laughed. Phokker, Mrs Spanner and Kitty sat in shocked silence at the incomprehensible conversation. "What?" asked Jack, now looking confused at them.

"Mmmph shiss phitt 'inn chikuns," said Dickens, and he left the room with a handful of greasy bacon he'd pilfered from the frying pan.

"What the fuck?" said Kitty.

"How the hell?" said Mrs Spanner.

"I'll rephrase that, Jack," said Phokker, "What was that all about, and how on Earth can you understand Dickens?"

"Easy," said Jack, and he carried on dunking his toast in to his egg.

"Well, what did he say about his tooth?" asked Mrs Spanner.

"Oh right," said Jack, "some weasels were chasing his chickens so he tried to bash them with his shovel."

"AND?" demanded Mrs Spanner.

"And he tripped over his prize turnip and the shovel hit him in the face, knocking out a tooth," answered Jack.

"But how do you understand what he's saying?" asked Phokker.

"The arm waving helps a lot," said Jack, "you got any more bacon, Mrs Spanner?" Phokker, Mrs Spanner and Kitty were all still totally confused, but seeing as Jack wasn't really helping or making any sense, they thought it best left alone for now. The clock chimed six.

"Chores to be done!" exclaimed Phokker, but Mrs Spanner insisted on everyone finishing breakfast first.

"They upstairs can wait a while longer," she said.

Lord Dickie and Her Ladyship were not exceptionally early risers, especially on a Saturday morning. And definitely not after they'd just had the Friday night from hell thrust upon them! Most of Lord Dickie's card nights ended in all being extremely drunk, so a lay in was always required. This, of course, suited Her Ladyship as she was often late back from the dog track. But not like last night. What the hell went wrong? What on Earth processed Sir Sidney Squirrel to jump out of the window? What will Dickens say when he sees his damaged roses? He'll go fucking mental! Anyways, let's crack on. While all the staff were busy with their chores, Lady Khuntingham was having another of her fabulous unicorn dreams. She was chasing it about the rose arbour. "Pinky! Pinky!" she called as it rounded a corner, but when she caught up with it, she became quite alarmed. Pinky had been trampled by a huge, black stallion with a long flowing mane. The creature was magnificent, with rippling muscles and fierce, hazel eyes. The stallion reared up and she could see its massive member.

"Pinky is dead," said the stallion, "he won't be returning." Her Ladyship was startled by the familiar voice but couldn't quite place it. She became nervous and tried to run.

She was frozen to the spot. (Funny those dreams ain't they? Where you can't move and it's all like really weird?) "Don't run, I won't hurt you," said the beautiful stallion. It came close and nuzzled into her ample bosoms.

"Oh my," she whimpered, as the horse became more and more amorous. She found herself becoming aroused and reached out to touch his dark mane. Their eyes met. "Oh, Phokker," she whispered, and the stallion started to lick her cleavage. She became moist.

"Morning, ma'am," said a girlish voice.

"Morning," she replied.

"What yer doing down there?" Suddenly, Her Ladyship was wide awake. There, standing above her was Kitty.

"GET OFF MY FUCKING BED!" shouted Her Ladyship.

"Yer on the bleedin' floor, yer silly cow!" Kitty yelled back and flung the curtains wide. The morning light streamed in and Her Ladyship winced at its brightness. She was very agitated at being woken up from such a strange but erotic dream.

"You ruined my dream!" she exclaimed.

"What was it about?" asked Kitty.

"Never you mind!" said Her Ladyship, "Just help me up." Kitty helped Her Ladyship to her feet but she was quite unsteady and walked her to the chaise under the window. Kitty noticed bruising around Her Ladyship's eyes and didn't know what to say.

She never thought in her wildest dreams that His Lordship was handy with his fists. Even though Her Ladyship could be a right bitch at times, he wouldn't smack her about, would he? Not a woman? "What's wrong?" asked Her Ladyship, "Why are you staring at me like that?" Kitty felt uncomfortable and looked at the floor. "Well? Answer me, girl!" demanded Her Ladyship. Kitty walked over to the dressing table, grabbed a small hand mirror and passed it gingerly to Her Ladyship.

"See for yerself," said Kitty, and she stepped back. Her Ladyship raised the looking glass and caught sight of her huge, puffy and bruised eyes.

"HOW THE FUCK AM I SUPPOSED TO HIDE THAT?" she screeched.

"Wiv a big hat," said Kitty meekly.

"INDOORS?" bellowed Her Ladyship. Kitty just stood and stared at her. It was silent for what seemed like an age. "I'll need shit loads of Papier Poudre on this!" cried Her Ladyship, finally breaking the silence. If you recall, she fell off the bench when she lunged at Phokker to kiss him and her nose broke her fall. On the floor. Big mess. Bless.

"Help me bathe and dress," she said to Kitty, "then we'll start the serious business of trying to cover up this fucking mess!"

"Yes, ma'am," said Kitty, and she went to prepare her bath in the adjacent room. She hoped that His Lordship wasn't becoming a cruel bastard and wife beater in his old age. He was too nice for that.

Phokker entered His Lordship's room with caution. It was time to rise, but seeing as everyone had gone to bed at stupid o'clock, he wondered if His Lordship was well rested and what type of mood he'd be in if he was not.

"Good morning, Phokker," said Lord Dickie as he watched Phokker creep across the room. Phokker was slightly startled, but not phased.

"Good morning, sir," said Phokker, "and how are we this morning, sir?"

"I feel amazing, my dear fellow," answered Lord Dickie.

"That's very good to hear, sir," said Phokker, as he opened the curtains. "it looks like it's going to be a beautiful day, sir."

"Is that so?" said His Lordship, "Then we shall all go to the seaside!" Phokker looked totally bemused. After the day and night that everyone had just had, this bloody idiot wanted to go to the seaside! Whatever next? "Well, what do you say, old chap?" asked Lord Dickie, "Are you up for some of that?"

"I…I…I don't know, sir," muttered Phokker, "I can't recall ever going to the seaside, sir."

Lord Dickie was quite taken aback at Phokker's statement. "Then we shall rectify that today!" he chortled, "Let the kitchen staff know they'll have to pack plenty of vittles'…and don't forget the gin!" His Lordship jumped out of bed and his wanger bounced about awaiting its usual bow tie. He looked down at his willy. "Not today," he said, "we're off to the seaside!" Phokker had no idea what had come over His Lordship, but he was glad to see that he was in fine form, if not a little too enthusiastic about the day ahead. He prepared His Lordship's bath and stood waiting with soap and loofah in his hands. "I can do that," said Lord Dickie, "you go and tell everyone that we're off to the seaside!" Phokker did as he was told and left the soap and loofah on the bath rack. His

Lordship climbed into the bath and picked up the loofah. *Now, what do I do with this thing?* he pondered.

Chapter Two

"The seaside!" exclaimed Mrs Spanner, "What the hell for?" Phokker picked up the cutlery and began to polish it up for the breakfast table. He could hear in Mrs Spanner's voice that she wasn't at all happy.

"His Lordship has decided that we shall all be visiting the seaside," said Phokker, "so a picnic, champagne and plenty of gin will be required."

"What about breakfast?" she moaned.

"We shall be leaving shortly after I assume," he replied, placing the cutlery into the lazy butler to send skywards to the dining room. "I shall get Jack to help me collect and pack the table and chairs." He headed upstairs to wallop the breakfast gong. It resonated about the hall and Lord Dickie came down looking a little flustered.

"Where on Earth do I put this?" he asked Phokker with one of his bow ties in his hand.

"You won't be requiring that for the seaside, sir," answered Phokker and placed it in his pocket. He held the door for His Lordship and seated him at the head of the table. Phokker retrieved the cutlery from the lazy butler set it in place.

"Do we have kippers?" Lord Dickie asked, "And my porridge?"

"I do believe so, sir," replied Phokker and His Lordship rubbed his hands together gleefully.

As Phokker was serving Lord Dickie his breakfast, he was looking at his attire for the day. He realised that a full tweed hunting suit would not be suitable for the seaside outing.

"I shall put your linen suit out for you after breakfast, sir," said Phokker.

"There's nothing wrong with this thing," said Lord Dickie.

"It would be fine for pheasant shooting, but not for taking the sea air, sir," Phokker said politely.

"You're quite right!" said His Lordship and stuffed his kipper into his mouth.

Her Ladyship was dressed but she and Kitty were having a few problems covering the bruises. "More powder," Lady Khuntingham said, "it needs more powder!"

"Yer gonna look like a bleedin' ghost if yer not careful," said Kitty. Lady Khuntingham picked up the powder puff and patted it furiously across her face. She dabbed rouge onto her lips and cheeks and thought she looked fine. "Yer look like yer going out to find some trade," said Kitty.

"How dare you!" Her Ladyship screeched. She looked into the mirror once more and realised that Kitty was right. She looked like a ho. She threw herself onto the bed and began to sob, rubbing her over-powdered face into the bed covers.

"I'll do it," said Kitty and sat Her Ladyship up on the side of her bed. She cleansed her face and started again.

Her Ladyship sat in a sulk the whole time and let out a little whimpering sob every now and then.

"'Ere, have a look," said Kitty, handing Her Ladyship the mirror. She held it up expecting to see the monstrous bruises staring back at her, but they were almost gone.

"Thank you, Kitty," her Ladyship smiled, "you're such a dear." She stood up and threw her shawl around her shoulders. "Let's go," she added and they walked down the stairs together. Her Ladyship turned left into the dining room and Kitty turned right to return to the kitchen below.

"Good morning, my dear," said Lord Dickie and rose from his chair to kiss his wife.

"What are you doing?" she asked him, completely taken aback at his early morning affections.

"We're off to the seaside today!" he said joyfully.

"We are fucking not!" she exclaimed.

Phokker made himself busy with the breakfast dishes and wondered if today was going to hit the shit fan any more than yesterday. They continued to argue and Phokker became more and more anxious. He dropped all the cutlery onto the floor and all went silent. Shivers of excitement ran up and down Her Ladyship's spine at the musical clattering metal. Phokker dropped to his knees and quickly set about picking it all up. Her Ladyship stooped to help, and her shawl slipped from her shoulders, revealing the top of her ripe, luscious mounds to Phokker. His groin ached.

She handed him the silverware and brushed against the back of his hand. His trousers were positively bulging!

"Are all the staff going to the seaside too?" she asked Lord Dickie, but looked into Phokker's hazel eyes as she did so.

"The more the merrier!" replied His Lordship.

"Then I shall need to wear something more suitable," she said, spinning around so to flick her hair in Phokker's direction. He could smell her distinctive perfume, *Eau du Lapin*, and he was fit to bursting, so he stood facing the sideboard to hide his throbbing truncheon.

"I shall be needing my linen suit too," Lord Dickie said to Phokker.

"I shall be along shortly," said Phokker, "so you may want to look at this morning's mail, sir." Lord Dickie followed his wife out into the hallway and patted her behind. She turned and smiled at him as she ascended the stairs. Phokker's groin ached and he realised that if he stayed facing the sideboard, he'd end up drilling a hole in it with his massive tool. He filled the lazy butler with all the breakfast dishes and sent it down to the kitchen. His knob was still ruling his head and it was distracting him terribly, so he sneaked up the back stairs and cracked one off in his room. His pent-up frustrations were relieved and he focused his attention on His Lordship's linen suit.

He hadn't wore it in quite some time; in fact, he hadn't worn it since they'd been in India.

Would it still fit him? Phokker pondered. He guessed it would as he'd always been portly but never obese. As Phokker removed it from the tallboy, he caught the feint whiff of antiseptic but thought nothing of it. The moth balls had

18

worked their magic as no holes were visible, but it was creased and would need pressing. He took it to Mrs Spanner. "Would it be possible for you to press His Lordship's suit?" asked Phokker.

"I'm still getting the bloody grub ready!" said Mrs Spanner, "Can't it wait?"

"Not really," answered Phokker, "it's His Lordship's outfit for the seaside.

"Fuckin' hells bells!" she growled, "Give it 'ere!" And she put the iron on to the range to heat up. She grabbed the garment from Phokker and he could see she was busy, but this really put her back up. He stepped towards the door.

"I'll be back in 20 minutes," he said.

"Bloody rush, rush, rush!" she blurted out. Phokker decided to see if Jack had finished polishing His Lordship's motor vehicle and retreated to the courtyard, leaving Mrs Spanner to her cursing.

Her Ladyship was still sifting through her wardrobe – hoping to find something suitable to wear.

She eventually found a dark blue gown with matching jacket and bonnet and rang the bell for Kitty's assistance. "What the bloody hell does she want now?" fumed Kitty as the bell on the kitchen wall rang out.

"Go and see what the silly cow wants and be back sharpish," said Mrs Spanner, pressing His Lordship's suit, "We still got loads to pack." Kitty flew up the back stairs and flung herself into Her Ladyship's room without knocking.

"What do you want now?" asked Kitty.

"I need your assistance dressing," said Her Ladyship.

"But yer dressed already!" said Kitty.

"Not for the seaside," barked Her Ladyship.

"Fuckin' hells bells!" stormed Kitty (she's been around Mrs Spanner far too long, as her language skills show!). Kitty undid all the buttons on the back of Her Ladyship's dress, helped her slip out of it, then put it aside. "I'm not changing yer corset too!" shrilled Kitty, "I got fings to get in wiv you know!" Her Ladyship gave a wry smile and stepped into the fresh gown. Kitty quickly fastened all the buttons and placed the old frock back into the wardrobe. "Anyfing else while I'm 'ere?" asked Kitty.

"That shall be all for now," said Her Ladyship and she shooed Kitty away. She sat at her dressing table and set about doing her hair.

Jack had polished the car and it shone like a new penny. He was very pleased with his work and knew His Lordship would be too.

"That's looking impressive, Jack," said Phokker, inspecting his work.

"Thanks, Phokker," replied Jack. He so wanted to ask Phokker about Molly but was afraid of the reaction he might get. "Er, can I ask you a question?" Phokker gave Jack a hard stare and wondered what on earth he was going to ask him. Jack could tell he was slightly agitated so changed his question. "Er...what do I need to wear to the seaside?" Jack asked. Phokker felt relief and gave Jack a straight answer.

"As staff, we shall be wearing what we would normally wear for our working day. You, however, shall require a hat as you are, after all, the chauffer," said Phokker.

Jack smiled as he had a hat at his mum's house. "Can I collect my hat on the way to the seaside?" asked Jack. "It's my army one, but that'll do, won't it?"

"That shall be sufficient until we're able to purchase a more suitable one," replied Phokker (eloquent ain't he!). He didn't see a problem with Jack collecting his hat, as long as his mother stayed indoors out of sight. "I shall inform His Lordship of our slight detour," said Phokker and left Jack to stare at the shiny motor vehicle.

Mrs Spanner had finished pressing His Lordship's suit and went back to packing the wicker picnic baskets with Kitty. Phokker came into the kitchen and before he could ask about the suit, Mrs Spanner pounced.

"It's over there," she said, pointing at the garment hung over the back of a chair.

"Thank you, Mrs Spanner," he said and took the suit to His Lordship's room.

"It didn't half pong," she said to Kitty.

"What of?" Kitty asked.

"Antiseptic," said Mrs Spanner, "very odd indeed."

"Who's auntie whats-it?" asked Kitty (thick as shit).

"No, no, antiseptic," said Mrs Spanner, "it's stuff you put on cuts. Doctors use it all the time."

"I ain't never been to a doctor," said Kitty.

"What, never?" asked Mrs Spanner.

"I don't fink so," said Kitty, "but I don't remember much of me being little, only me ever being 'ere."

"You was lucky Dickens found you at all," said Mrs Spanner.

"How come?" asked Kitty. Mrs Spanner went on to explain that Dickens was an alcoholic. Was; until the day he found Kitty crawling about in the mud between the cabbages. He would often stumble about, crushing lettuces and onions with a bottle of cheap gin in his hands, shouting obscenities at his chickens for being under his feet.

However, the sight of a grubby child, crawling through the cabbages in just a tatty old night shirt, shook him up so much that he stopped drinking that very day. He said it was 'a sign from God' that saved him.

That was when he was a lot more coherent in speech, of course; since then, he'd lost so many teeth (and with only his chickens for company in the old folly), his state of mind and dialect had all but left him 'unstable'.

"Gin is a sin," scoffed Mrs Spanner, who had seen many succumb to its evil ways. Kitty knew of Her Ladyship's gin snorting secret but didn't say anything. In those days it was an arrestable offence and even though Her Ladyship could be a right bitch at times, she wouldn't see her locked up for it. His Lordship would suffer greatly too if her sordid little secret ever came to light. Luckily, all evidence of that had been wiped out of existence only yesterday. Just like Quithers; whatever happened to him? Anyway, Kitty kept schtum.

Chapter Three

Phokker and Jack loaded the wicker picnic baskets onto the back of His Lordship's motor vehicle (they had a proper rack for those things back then). As they returned to the kitchen for a cup of tea, they were met with a stern look from Mrs Spanner. "Where's this one bleedin' goin' then?" she asked, pointing to a huge basket on the floor.

"We don't have room for that," replied Phokker.

"Then them posh arses will either be standin' up or sat on the sand," said Mrs Spanner, "This is the table 'n' chairs!" They took that sort of thing with them whenever and wherever they went on a picnic. The staff would carry it and set it all up. His Lordship's late mother once had her old staff carry it to the summit of Mount Snowden and she moaned like fuck because her tea had 'gone cold'. What a real bitch she was!

"You shall have to follow in the horse and cart with Dickens, Kitty and the basket, I'm afraid," said Phokker, "as there's no room for all of us in His Lordship's motor vehicle."

"I ain't goin'!" stormed Mrs Spanner.

"We are ALL going at His Lordship's request," said Phokker with mastery in his tone.

"Bollocks!" said a miserable-looking Mrs Spanner.

Kitty stood clapping her hands and cheering like a demented seal. She, like Phokker, had never been to the seaside and she was really excited.

"Does Dickens know that he's goin' too?" asked Mrs Spanner.

"I shall go and speak with him now," said Phokker, "but I'll need Jack to translate what he's saying." They left the kitchen with a gloomy Mrs Spanner and a blissfully happy Kitty.

His Lordship felt a little squeezed in his linen suit, but knew that Phokker had made the right choice of attire; much better choice than he himself had made earlier. He returned to the study to finish reading the morning's mail and still he could see that nothing had arrived from India. His heart was heavy from the lack of contact but knew, deep down, that Bunnitta had obviously moved on. A lost love (lust more like!). As he flicked through, he found an envelope which had no postage stamp on. It merely stated in the top right-hand corner, where His Majesty's noble head would normally perch, two words: 'HAND DELIVERED'. He opened it to find the child-like scribbles of Doctor Foster. A quick note to say that Sir Sidney Squirrel had been sedated overnight and that he would be having a full psychoanalysis that very day. Electric shock treatment, immersive wave treatment, hypnosis and even a blancmange enema! His Lordship winced as he read the almost endless list of dreadful things that awaited Sir Sidney that day. "Poor old bugger," said His Lordship, "that blancmange stuff gets everywhere!"

Phokker and Jack found Dickens, sat on the steps of the old folly, feeding his chickens. His cloth cap was pulled down low so he didn't see them approaching. "Hello there, Dickens," said Phokker.

"Wha the fugginhellis goin' on?" yelled Dickens. Phokker looked at Jack.

"Do you want polite translation or more accuracy?" Jack asked Phokker.

"Polite, please," said Phokker.

"How can I help you?" Jack translated (very diplomatic!).

"Can you take the horse and cart to the seaside today, please?" asked Phokker.

"Wha the mmmph crumple ya wanna ummf bloody zeezide?" said Dickens.

"Why the seaside," translated Jack.

"His Lordship would like a day at the seaside and has requested that all staff attend," explained Phokker.

"'Orse 'n' cart will mmmph not bein' ffmmph crumple arse," replied Dickens.

23

"Oh, deary me," said Jack nervously.

"Be very careful what you say," said Phokker.

"It appears that he doesn't want to go," said Jack.

"I shall give you a pound if you do," said Phokker, removing said note from his waistcoat, waving it in Dickens' face. Dickens shot up quick smart and grabbed the note from Phokker's hand, scaring his chickens in the process.

They scattered about, bumping into each other, with feathers flying everywhere. Dickens darted off to the stables and prepared Moses the horse. He attached the swingletree and gently drew the cart up behind the horse. He then led Moses out to where Phokker and Jack were stood, covered in feathers and chicken shit. "That was quick!" said Phokker.

"I don't be mmmph fungle crump futchin' much ya noes!" laughed Dickens.

"I know," Jack translated.

"Meet us in the courtyard in ten minutes," said Phokker, who looked down at himself and then at Jack. "We best change out of these first!" he said.

Her Ladyship was wondering how to place her bonnet on her huge piled-up mane. She wanted to look graceful and elegant for the sake of her husband but she also wanted to look ravishingly beautiful for Phokker. "Oh, fuck it!" she said to herself, "Kitty can help me with it later." She went downstairs and sat in the drawing room. She picked at the tiny flowers that adorned the back of her lace gloves while she waited. And waited. And waited. "Good lord, this is fucking boring!" she said and decided to see if her husband was still in his study.

"I told you to kno…"

"It's me, dear, so I doubt very much I have to knock in my own home," said Her Ladyship, cutting her husband off dead.

"Are we ready to go yet?" she asked him, "I'm awfully bored just sat waiting around." His Lordship opened a window and called out to Phokker. But no reply. He called out to Jack. Nothing. He rang the bell pull. No one came.

"Where is everybody?" he asked in frustration. Phokker came rushing into the room with his attire not looking its normal, tidy self.

"What are you up to, old boy?" asked Lord Dickie.

"We had a problem with Dickens' chickens," replied Phokker, "but it has now been resolved, sir."

"Good, good," said Lord Dickie.

"If you wait out the front, sir, I shall have Jack drive round to meet you both," said Phokker as he finished buttoning up his waistcoat and jacket. Her Ladyship couldn't take her eyes off Phokker as he fumbled about with the buttons. She so wanted to tell him not to bother but she knew this would aggrieve both men. She lusted after him and she wanted him. And by her short and curlies, she was going to have him. Again.

Jack helped Dickens with putting the large wicker basket onto the cart by the time Phokker reached the kitchen.

Mrs Spanner was still very annoyed that she had to go to the seaside. She HATED the seaside. It reminded her too much of her husband Joe when they were courting.

He'd often taken her on the pier and the bandstand but they got in trouble for doing that when they were caught by Constable Mistlethwaite. Joe called him 'Misertwat' on purpose, and got a smack round the ear for saying it. "I can't help it," Joe explained, "I got a terrible lithsp cuntsthable." Joe received many smacks round the ear for being cheeky to the police, but it was all his own fault. He just couldn't keep his mouth shut around them and his gob filter totally disappeared. At least Mrs Spanner wasn't having to take Joe with her. This, you may have thought, would slightly cheer her up, but memories linger like a scotch egg fart in the dark. Rotten.

"Are you ready Mrs Spanner?" asked Phokker.

"As ready as I'll ever be," she replied.

"Where's Kitty?" he asked.

"She's been sat on that bleedin' cart ever since Dickens brought it in the courtyard!" she replied.

"Good," Phokker said, "let's be off then." Mrs Spanner left the comfort of her kitchen and looked like a sulky-arsed badger who'd munched on too many sour worms. Phokker locked the door and helped Mrs Spanner onto the back of the cart. Kitty was still in hand-clapping, demented seal mode, which annoyed Mrs Spanner further.

"Will you shut the fuck up?" demanded Mrs Spanner.

"Can I sit up front wiv you, Dickens?" Kitty asked.

"Course mmmph crumpet fffmph lovely titz," replied Dickens with a filthy grin.

"I'll take that as a yes then," said Kitty and she made her way up to the front.

"Better than sittin' next to that miserable ol' cow!" Dickens' grin widened as he snapped the reigns to make Moses move. He glanced down at Kitty's wobbly mounds as the cart rumbled across the cobble-stoned courtyard. It was like watching two huge jellies trying to escape their far too small moulds. Dickens was happier than a cockerel in a horny hen house!

Phokker had sent Dickens and the women on ahead as it was more than likely they'd have a much slower journey in the cart. He watched them leave and wondered why Mrs Spanner had a face like a smacked backside. Why on earth did she look so glum? A day at the seaside would brighten her spirits and get her out of that smoky kitchen. She should feel well chuffed at going out for the day! He gave a hefty tug on the starting handle and the car leapt into life. It shuddered and juddered over the cobble stones and then drew up near the front entrance.

"What the fucking hell is that?" Her Ladyship demanded.

"That's me new motor vehicle, dearest," replied His Lordship.

"Where's the horses and carriage?" she shrieked in a high pitch tone that probably only rabid wolves could hear.

"We're going in style!" said Lord Dickie proudly.

"I'm not going anywhere in that fucking thing!" she yelled and crossed her arms in determination.

Phokker opened the back door and waited for them to climb aboard. Lady Khuntingham was having none of it.

"Come on, my dear," said Lord Dickie, "don't be a sulky pants." This infuriated her even more. Phokker pretended that he couldn't see or hear what was going on between them.

Jack, on the other hand, was far too conspicuous as he was staring at them, having their full-blown tiff, with his gob wide open.

"Stop catching flies, Jack," whispered Phokker, "you look like a codfish."

"Sorry," said Jack, slightly blushing. He turned and faced the steering wheel, trying his best to look uninterested, but he just looked constipated. Phokker coughed loudly over the rowing couple and they looked at him.

"Are we ready, sir?" asked Phokker.

"Well I am, old boy," said Lord Dickie and he rushed down the steps and jumped into the back of the car.

"You're going to leave me here?" bellowed Her Ladyship. "ON MY OWN!"

"Go and see if Her Ladyship's coming, Phokker," asked His Lordship. Phokker walked up the steps and held out his hand to her. He looked deep into her eyes and she into his. Her heart was pounding in her chest and his groin was seeking a rampant reward.

Phokker leaned forward and spoke softly. "Please," he said. Just one word. She took his hand and he guided her down the steps and into the back of the car. Phokker climbed in next to Jack and with one swift hand movement from him, the car lurched forward. Lady Khuntingham gave a loud shriek and Lord Dickie tried to comfort her. She slapped his hand away and she gripped the seat as tightly as she could. Her sullen look pissed off His Lordship and he turned to look out of the window, wondering if the sulky-arsed bitch was going to be like this all the way. He hoped not, or the gin in the onboard cocktail cabinet would be gulped down quicker than a toothless, skanky ho giving her trade a gummy gobble.

Chapter Four

Mrs Spanner was still grumbling away on the back of the cart and it started to annoy Kitty. "What cha moanin' about, Queenie?" asked Kitty. Mrs Spanner threw Kitty one of her 'looks' to shut her up but it didn't work. "Don't be grumpy, Queenie," said Kitty, "we'll have a lovely day at the seaside."

"Lovely!" scoffed Mrs Spanner, "What's so bleedin' lovely about it?" Kitty couldn't really explain why as she'd never been to the seaside before, but she was looking forward to it so much that she could hardly contain her excitement. This was noticed by Dickens and he had the biggest grin on his face as she bounced up and down next to him.

"Mmmph crumple mmrgh pherzz zeazide mmph an' titz," mumbles Dickens with his almost toothless grin.

"What?" said Kitty as she tried her best to try and decipher all the syllables excreting from Dickens' gob. But to no avail. She gave up. "I'm going back to check on Queenie," Kitty said.

"Aww, must ye, lovely arze?" Dickens said sullenly. She carefully turned and climbed into the back of the cart and Dickens began to sulk.

He was hoping that her voluptuous bosoms would pop out while going down Wigton Way but no such luck. Kitty sat opposite Mrs Spanner, who was resting her elbows on the wicker basket, propping up her miserable head.

"What's wrong Queenie?" she asked.

"I bleedin' hates the seaside," Mrs Spanner replied, "Too many bad memories." Mrs Spanner went into great detail about her courting days with Joe and all the trouble they'd gotten into.

Kitty frowned. "But that was years ago, Queenie," said Kitty, "Why don't cha just let it be?"

"I can't just un-remember, you know!" sulked Mrs Spanner.

"Please try, or you'll make everyone bleedin' miserable!" Kitty said, rubbing Mrs Spanner's arm. But she continued to sulk. Kitty looked back to see where the others were but had no sighting of them. Dickens sat with a face that looked like it had been slapped with a week-old kipper; only he was smellier.

Lady Khuntingham still had her vice-like grip on the seat and Lord Dickie was on his second large gin and tonic. Jack was still nervous but took directions from Phokker. Both were glad that His Lord and Ladyship were partitioned off from them as Jack's bum squeaked and billowed noxious gases through his anxiety. Phokker got a handkerchief from his pocket to cover his nose from Jack's pong-whiffy arse.

The scent of *Eau de Lapin* wafted up his hooter and he realised it was his monkey spanking hanky (the one he used to mop Her Ladyship's brow with after their liaison in the dining room).

He stiffened and looked around to see if he could catch Her Ladyship's gaze, but all he saw was His Lordship guzzling back the gin. His trousers were stretching slightly and his groin ached for more of Her Ladyship. He momentarily lost concentration and Jack nearly took a wrong turn. "Not that way!" Phokker shouted as he broke out of his daydream. "That'll take us over Bottom's Bridge...and we don't want to go THAT way!" As you may recall, that's where Deathwatch Lil had removed Quithers from the back of His Lordship's car after the cad was caught almost trying to blackmail Her Ladyship. I wonder what Deathwatch Lil has done with him? Anyway...Jack gulped at recalling his fateful journey with Phokker the evening before, and his bum clenched tighter than a Scotsman's wallet.

"We're nearly at Mum's house," said Jack, "Have you told His Lordship we're stopping off to get my hat?" Phokker had completely forgotten to mention it and felt very annoyed with himself.

"Pull up outside and I shall inform His Lordship," said Phokker.

Jack rounded the corner by the church and pulled up outside his mum's house. Phokker got out, walked around the back of the car and opened the door. "I'm so sorry, sir," said Phokker, "I should have informed you earlier but Jack is just collecting his hat."

"That's OK, old boy," said His Lordship, "I'll just get out and stretch me legs a bit." In reality he was hoping that a crowd would gather round his car so he could show it off. There was no one in sight. Her Ladyship was sat there, facing the front, with an iron-like grip on the seat. She was in a state of shock; still. Jack got out and opened the garden gate.

"Don't be long," called Phokker, "and keep your mother inside, for heaven's sake!" Jack gave a thumb's up and went indoors. His Lordship strolled around the outside of his new motor vehicle and he was very pleased with himself. He saw someone waving from the front of the church. It was the Right Reverend, Newton Dimplebum. An honourable man named after Sir Issac Newton. Dimplebum, however, was a long-standing family name; been around for centuries. First given to the court physicians in the eleventh century by William the Conqueror, derived from 'Ladies having dimply skin across the thighs and buttocks' (we call it cellulite these days!).

A week's course of bleeding by leeches was usually required, but they used leeches like they were going out of fashion back then! So, the name Dimplebum has been around for a long time. Anyway, I digress once again…His Lordship wandered over to the church to have a chat. Phokker was alone with Her Ladyship; at last.

"Mum! Mum!" called Jack, "Where's my army hat?" Jack's mother came out of the kitchen with her fish gut-drenched apron on, blood and fish snot dripping all over the linoleum.

"Oh, yer back then?" she asked him.

"No, I'm just getting my hat," he replied and dashed upstairs to his room. He fumbled about in the wardrobe and found it being crushed by the weight of his old army boots. He punched the top of his hat outwards and gave the buttons a quick spit and polish.

"So, where 'ave you been ALL night?" asked his mother, standing at the bottom of the stairs with her grotty hands resting on her huge hips.

"I'm working for His Lordship now," he answered.

"Well the extra money will come in handy," she said.

"Oh, I won't be living here," explained Jack, "I have a room up at the Abbey."

"What shall I do without your money?" she squealed.

"I'm not here, so you don't have to feed me," he said.

"But what about the money?" she squealed again.

"Why don't you take in another lodger?" asked Jack. His mother thought about this for a few seconds.

"When can yer shift yer stuff out?" she asked.

"Wow! Talk about getting rid of your only son quick!"

Jack scoffed in amazement. "Well…when?" she asked again (bloody cheek of the woman).

"Not today," he said, "we're off to the seaside today."

The kettle whistled and his mother went to take it off the boil. "You'll have a cuppa with yer ol' mum before yer go?" she asked and Jack followed her into the kitchen.

Meanwhile, Phokker was staring at Her Ladyship's ashen face in the back of the car. He looked across and Lord Dickie had disappeared into the church with the Reverend. Phokker climbed into the back of the car and sat next to her.

"Are you all right, ma'am?" he asked her. She was white with shock. He prized her hands from the seat and rubbed with his great hairy shovels to try and bring hers back to life. She turned her head slowly and stared him in the eyes.

"What…the…fuck…is…this…thing?" she murmured.

"His Lordship's new motor vehicle arrived yesterday, ma'am," he explained, "But you were otherwise incapacitated in your room if you recall."

"But where's my beautiful carriage?" she whimpered with her eyes welling up. "And the horses?"

"They are still in the stables, ma'am," he answered, "All quite safe." Her hands were coming back to life and pins and needles started to pinch at the end of her fingers.

"They're all tingly," she said, lifting up both hands to Phokker's face. He kissed the end of each of her delicate digits and she closed her eyes in bliss. He gently folded his huge fingers in between hers and pulled her towards him swiftly. Their noses touched. "Ouch!" she simpered.

"Still hurts, does it?" he asked.

"Only a little," she replied.

He tilted his head slightly to the right and kissed her sweet rosebud lips. Her mound of Venus began to throb and his trouser truncheon was trying to fight its way out by stretching the material to its maximum.

"I want you," she whispered.

"But how?" he asked.

"Oh, just fucking take me!" she growled, as she bent over the seat and started to hoist up her dress and numerous petticoats. Phokker wasted no time in releasing his massive manhood and shoved it right up her!

She placed her lace gloves over her mouth for fear of her moans of pleasure being heard. Phokker gripped her hips tighter and tighter as he pounded away. Her peachy arse made his stroke quicken and he so wanted to go down to taste her deliciousness, but he'd save that for another time. He furtively kept a watch all the while but his gaze kept coming back to her rounded rump. The car rocked from side to side. She let out a muffled squeal from behind her lace gloves and he unloaded all his pent-up frustrations. He withdrew and wiped his meat with one of her many petticoats and put himself away.

He then helped her put all her under garments back into place and sat her back on the seat. She was extremely relaxed and sat grinning inanely.

"And so, shall ye not covet thy neighbour's ass," Reverend Dimplebum finished.

"So, that's tomorrow's sermon I take it?" Lord Dickie asked, "Covering neighbour's arses?"

"No, no, my dear fellow," said the Reverend, "Covet: to desire something that one does not possess and belongs to another." Lord Dickie tried so very hard to stifle a yawn and looked at his pocket watch.

"Is that the time? Must dash," said His Lordship, "See you tomorrow morning!" And he made a swift exit from the church. The Reverend strolled back towards the vestry and caught the cleaner on all fours.

"What are you doing, Mrs Merrywither?" he enquired.

"Rubbin' me brass," she replied, but he misheard.

"You're as bad as His Lordship!" he said with a shocked expression. "I suggest you go outside for your rubbings!"

His Lordship got back into the car to find his wife in an almost horizontal position, looking *non compos mentis*. "Are you all right, me dear?" he quizzed. She simply let out a girlish giggle and drooled slightly.

"Have you been at the gin?" he asked, checking the bottle. "I knew a stiff one would sort you out."

She giggled again and as Phokker closed the door, he murmured. "How right you are, sir!"

Jack said bye from the front door. He didn't want his mother giving him a hug or a kiss or he'd smell like fish guts all day. He'd just closed the gate when his mother came out to wave him off. Jack quickly jumped into the driver's seat and beckoned Phokker to turn the starting handle. "I told you to keep your mother indoors!" shouted Phokker. He turned the handle; nothing. Jack's mother was now at the gate. He turned the handle again; still nothing. She walked towards the car. Phokker violently turned the handle and the car sprang to life.

It jiggled and jostled, frightening Jack's mother so much that she fainted and fell backwards over the garden wall.

"Leave her, Jack," said Phokker, "she's a hard woman – she'll be fine." Jack pulled away but looked over his shoulder to make sure his mother was OK. "Careful," yelled Phokker, "you'll run the postie over!" Jack steered away from the postie who dismounted his bike quicker than a jockey needing a piss at the end of a race. They sped off (seven miles an hour was considered 'speed' back then!) and drove on to Wigton Way. The postie was slightly shaken so he pushed up his bike.

He came to Jack's mother's house and perched his bike against the wall. He peered over to see Jack's mother flat on her back, legs akimbo, showing everything God gave her (and much more besides!).

"I see you have a new post box, Mrs Proudfoot," said the postie and he promptly dropped the mail into her slot.

Chapter Five

Kitty was trying to cheer Mrs Spanner up as the cart jostled through Piddleton. She was singing songs, trying to get the miserable old cow to join in, but she still sat there with a face that looked like it had been slapped with a rancid, dead fish (oh of course, it had been hadn't it – her husband smacked her about with a dead poached pike!).

"Why you bein' such a gnashbag, Queenie?" asked Kitty. "You're making me miserable too, you knows!" Mrs Spanner sighed a weary sigh and looked at her. She suddenly realised they were passing through Piddleton, and a small, wry smile lifted the corner of her mouth as they passed the town hall. "My cream puffs were legendary there," said Mrs Spanner.

"Yes, I remember you telling me," said Kitty. The horse and cart rumbled along the cobbles and as they neared St. Dominics Church, Mrs Spanner could see the familiar, messy, ginger mop of the vicar standing out front. She tapped Dickens' shoulder and asked him to pull up.

"Mummmph grumfle mmph asrey what?" he moaned.

"Just stop 'ere!" she demanded, "I've unfinished business with the vicar (the man who fathered her sister's five kids and abandoned them when she passed over)." She leapt swiftly from the cart, like an injured gazelle with a new found vigour…or was it anger? Revenge?

She flew through the churchyard and blindsided the vicar, who for a fleeting moment, didn't recognise her. She was almost lost for words as rage took over her and she grabbed him by the Trossachs. His eyes bulged and his mouth gaped wide, expelling the most ear-piercing scream you could ever imagine, so much so, that nearby dogs started to bark and howl.

35

"Now I got yer attention, I'll be saying me piece," she snarled, "so best you be listening well good and proper." The vicar's eyes streamed and he nodded slowly. "You knows who I am?" she asked. He nodded. "Good," she hissed through gritted teeth. "You were cruel to my sister and let her kids, YOUR kids, go when she passed away. I brought um up with a great deal of struggle and sacrifice and I finks you need to help pay for all your past indiscretions, don't you?" He nodded once again. "I'll be back this way later and you better have something worthwhile for me to collect," she said, "Or these 'ere tallywags will be ripped off and shoved down yer cake 'ole!" Her grip tightened and searing pain made his nose start to bleed. She let him go and he dropped to his knees, clutching his wounded tackle. She spun round and jumped back up onto the cart just as swiftly as she'd leapt from it. As Dickens pulled away, she stared hard at her victim. "I'll be back!" she yelled and let out a triumphant laugh.

"That were amazing, Queenie!" said Kitty, really chuffed, "He'll be nursing them for days!"

Mrs Spanner was well impressed with herself and smiled broadly. "That's made my day that has!" she grinned. "Let's get a move on, Dickens!" He was gob-smacked that Mrs Spanner's vice-like grip brought a man to his knees and told himself never to mess with her. The vicar crawled slowly towards the rectory; with every movement, stabbing pain seared through his groin.

He called out to his wife. "Franny! Franny! I need some ice for Mr Jolly and his boiled eggs!"

Jack was growing ever more accustomed to His Lordship's car and seemed far less nervous by the lack of smells his bottom was omitting. For this, Phokker was in deep, silent gratitude. They passed through Wigton Way's steep, main street, with looks of shock from some and admiration from others. This was noted by His Lordship and it made him very happy. He was waving at everyone, but as the back of the car was surrounded by wood, metal and very little glass, they could hardly see him. And boy, did he want to be seen! "Can I sit up front?" he called out, but it was slightly muffled. He knocked on the glass partition between them and Phokker turned around.

"Slow down, Jack," said Phokker, "I think His Lordship wants something." Jack slowed right down – a whole three miles an hour, but still His Lordship couldn't be heard. Jack pulled over at Phokker's command and the car sat melodically chuffing away.

"I'd like to sit up front," Lord Dickie said.

"Where shall I sit, sir?" asked Phokker.

"You can keep Her Ladyship company," Lord Dickie replied. "She's in no fit state at the moment, so it'll be quiet." Phokker didn't really need to be asked twice and sprang from his seat to swap places. Jack was nervous but Phokker told him to relax and not let it bother him. There were plenty of road signs to follow and he was sure that His Lordship would help him along the way. Then they were off again towards Piddleton. His Lordship asked Jack to drive slowly through the town so all could see his beautiful new motor vehicle. Some leapt out of the way in horror and some waved. Lord Dickie waved vigorously at everyone.

Lady Khuntingham threw Phokker an extremely saucy look as soon as he got in the back of the car and his groin twitched (gets going so easily!). She slid her hand across the seat and toyed with the thick, dark hair on the back of his huge hand. "You'll get us in trouble," Phokker whispered.

"He's more interested in what others think of him and this thing," she said, "Anyway, they can't hear us."

"But what if he turns round?" asked Phokker nervously.

"Look at him," she scoffed, "he's happier than a dog with two dicks!" Phokker knew she was right, but still his nerves were getting the better of him. She moved closer and placed her hand on his knee, rubbing it gently. His trouser snake shook wildly and she could see his monster dancing in his trousers. That impressed her greatly. She manoeuvred her hand up his meaty thigh and squeezed it cheekily.

"If this thing escapes," he said, pointing to his groin, "it'll end up redecorating the roof!"

She licked her lips, like a tiger getting ready to devour its prey. "I'm tired and need to lie down," she said.

"Then I shall move out of your way," said Phokker.

"You fucking won't!" she insisted, "You stay right there!" And she lay her head in his lap. She faced towards him and started to undo his trouser buttons. He grabbed at her hand to stop her, but as she looked up at him with her doe eyes, he could not resist – he let her continue. His beast was released and it almost took her eye out. Her soft, rosebud lips surrounded its tip and she started to suck. She had more suction than Hubert Cecil Booth's vacuum cleaner! It didn't take long for Phokker to unload, as her sucking and the car's jostling brought him off quicker than he'd have liked. She sat up and searched her handbag for his face powder, as if nothing had occurred between them. He was left to do himself up and she patted her face delicately.

"I fink I can see His Lordship's motor fingy," said Kitty pointing back.

"I finks yer right, my girl," said Mrs Spanner. Kitty started to wave.

"Coo-ee, Jack!" she shouted.

"Sit down, silly girl, or you'll fall out!" shouted Mrs Spanner.

"I was only waving," Kitty sulked. The car came closer and closer and overtook them slowly.

"Kin stooped mmph bazturds grumflr mmumph twats!" shouted Dickens, all afraid. Mrs Spanner noticed that His Lordship was sat up front and wondered where Phokker was. He turned and waved from the small back window.

"Well I never!" Mrs Spanner exclaimed.

"You never what?" asked Kitty.

"Never you mind!" retorted Mrs Spanner.

They rounded the corner but His Lordship's car was trailing off into the distance and up over the hill.

"We best take the shortcut, Dickens," said Mrs Spanner, "We don't want to wear Moses outgoing up over that 'ill."

Dickens pulled the reins slightly to the left and they followed the old track road. It was a little winding, but was used less often these days, so they could make good progress. "We'll be there in no time at all now," said Mrs Spanner, and Kitty went back in to hand-clapping-demented-seal mode. Mrs Spanner just shook her head.

As Jack reached the brow of the hill, Saltbury-On-Sea, in all its glory, could be seen. The sea glistened like a million jewels and the sea air touched His Lordship's nostrils. "Ah, nothing better!" he said as he took in a deep breath. Jack sniffed the air but all he could smell was the oily car.

"Er, yes, sir," said Jack, "nothing like it at all." His Lordship's hand reached over his shoulder and he tapped on the glass partition.

"Nearly there, me dear," he shouted over the engine. She merely smiled and waved weakly. Phokker went pale at the thought of them being caught but he was well clear of all her naughtiness. He hadn't brought a clean pair of trousers with him, so it was a good job his sphincter clenched tightly or he'd have stank all day. They drove past cottages, then houses and shops, until they reached the seafront.

"Where shall I stop, sir?" asked Jack.

"Down there, my boy," said His Lordship pointing, "I can see other motor vehicles parked up." Jack drove along and pulled up behind two others cars. The rest of the seafront was filled with horses with their carriages and plenty of bicycles. The car came to a jolting stop and Her Ladyship squealed once again. She loved to over dramatize things and you'd think that after her shafting and gobbling, she'd be well and truly relaxed! Phokker got out, opened the door and helped Her Ladyship out of the car.

She gave him a sly wink and he stifled a cheeky grin. "Shall we promenade?" she asked her husband.

"A good idea," he answered and she took his arm to walk along the front.

"We shall wait here for the others to arrive, sir," said Phokker, "I shall come and inform you when we're all set up, sir."

"Tally-ho!" said His Lordship and off they strolled.

Jack got out and his legs felt like jelly. He gripped the side of the car as his pins shook. "You'll have to get used to it, Jack," said Phokker.

"I will," replied Jack, "still early days!"

Promenading along the seafront, Her Ladyship knew that wearing such a bold, dark colour in early May was a risky move (a total fashion faux pas back then!), but she didn't give a shit and liked all the attention she received from the other ladies. Gentlemen stared at her in admiration and this made Lord Dickie very proud – knowing his wife was beautiful and could still turn lusting heads around. She'd be beating them off with a shitty stick if he wasn't there and he knew it! The cart slowly came around the corner and drew up with all the other carts at the far end of the seafront. Them that were lowly enough to remember their place in society, knew that they wouldn't be welcome to park down with the hoity toity posh gits in their carriages, let alone them shiny new motor vehicles!

Kitty ran down, waving all the time to Jack. She gave him an impressive squeeze.

"I missed you," she whispered.

"I only just left you at the house!" he said.

"But that was AGES ago!" she purred and ran her fingers across his chest. He coughed and shook himself.

"Well I guess we best unload these," he said, releasing himself from Kitty's grip. Phokker and Jack unloaded the wicker baskets and placed them on the promenade, while Kitty stood watch, waiting for Mrs Spanner and Dickens. They found a comfortable spot on the beach and took the wicker baskets down the steps. Kitty took off her shoes and stockings as she wanted to know how the sand would feel between her toes.

"It's all warm," she said, rubbing her feet through the sand.

"Best not let them toffs see you doin' that, my girl!" shouted Mrs Spanner from the top of the steps. "You knows your place, so keep them shoes on!"

"I only wanted to…" Kitty started.

"SHOES ON!" Mrs Spanner snapped back and Kitty began to sulk; again. Dickens had carried the largest wicker basket all the way down on his shoulders. He may have been a slight man, but he was as strong as an ox. Jack and Phokker helped him carry it down the steps and Kitty helped Mrs Spanner set up the table and chairs.

They removed cups, saucers, tea pots and the such from another basket and placed them on top of a crisp white tablecloth. Phokker pumped the kerosene in the primus stove and lit it, placing a huge copper kettle on top. Mrs Spanner and Kitty opened the food basket and Dickens began to drool. "Mmuph crusty gumph pherr piez?" Dickens said.

"Could he have a pie, please?" said Jack, deciphering Dickens. Mrs Spanner gave Dickens a huge slice of gala pie and he began to suck away (he only has two teeth remember!). His disgusting manners made Kitty cringe and she turned away from him; revolting. The table was set and everyone stood by.

"I shall go and tell His Lordship we are ready," said Phokker and he strolled along the promenade searching for them. He was quite lost until he caught sight of Her Ladyship's dark gown, swishing from side to side. He knew just what was under there and he wanted more. A lot more. He walked around and then paused in front of them.

"Tiffin is served, sir," he said.

"Good show!" said His Lordship and they turned and walked back, not discussing anything in particular, just gently waving and tipping his hat to the other gentry. Phokker followed and watched Her Ladyship's arse sway. She knew exactly what she was doing and Phokker's trousers groaned. He marched in front to lead the way and to (hopefully?) stop his growing member from exploding in his pants.

When they reached their spot on the beach, Phokker seated them both while Mrs Spanner and Kitty poured the tea. "Where's Quithers?" Her Ladyship asked. Lord Dickie looked at Phokker. Phokker looked at Jack. Jack looked at them both and his bum squeaked loudly.

"I didn't know they had mice at the seaside!" Her Ladyship laughed. The three just stood staring at each other. What on earth could they tell her?

Chapter Six

As the tiffin was coming to an end, His Lordship could hear a fuss way up on the promenade. He stood and glanced over to where his shiny motor car was parked and could see a small crowd all gathering around it. He went, in a huff, to wave them off, but realised that he knew some of the gentlemen standing there. "I'm just popping up to chat to some old chums of mine, me dear," he said to his wife. She gave him a forced smile and put her hand out, expecting him to kiss the back of it. He ignored it totally as he was too transfixed by the chaps who were ogling his latest acquisition.

"If you need to discuss anything about the motor vehicle, sir, there is an information booklet in the cocktail cabinet," said Phokker.

"By Jove, that's marvellous!" grinned Lord Dickie and off he went with a merry spring in his step. Mrs Spanner and Kitty were clearing the table while Jack started to pack away His Lordship's chair.

"We shall require that again for luncheon," said Phokker, "so best not put it away just yet."

"We got to stay for that too?" moaned Jack.

"All day, if necessary," replied Phokker.

"Bloody hell!" mumbled Jack, not delighted at the very prospect of staying there ALL day! Mrs Spanner heard what Phokker had said, and started to look glum once more.

"Cheer up, Queenie," said Kitty with a smile.

"Bugger off!" Mrs Spanner growled.

"Surely, you can't still be miserable about the old times?" asked Kitty.

"I 'kin be as miserable as I likes about the old days!" Mrs Spanner snorted. Kitty wasn't going to let Mrs Spanner's

43

gloomy experiences of the seaside dampen her first ever visit to the seaside and decided to ignore her altogether. They packed away the tiffin things in silence. Phokker watched the pair exchanging dagger-like glances at each other as they tidied up and wondered what on Earth was going on between them. Did he dare ask? Or would he just be told to fuck off? He expected the latter from the pair of them and decided to stay well out of it.

"I'm bloody bored," said Her Ladyship.

"Why not go and join His Lordship, ma'am?" asked Phokker.

"Oh, fuck me, no," exclaimed Her Ladyship, "That'll bore me to tears even more!" She stood and straightened out her crumpled dress, lifting her lace parasol with a swift movement, and walked towards the steps.

"So, you've decided to join your husband?" asked Phokker.

"Fuck, no," she replied, "I'm off to promenade."

"On your own?" asked Phokker, aghast.

"Unless you'd care to join me?" she asked back, holding out her lace-gloved hand.

Mrs Spanner knew exactly what Lady Khuntingham was up to and thought she better nip it in the bud bloody quick!

"Phokker," called Mrs Spanner, "we could do with your help 'ere actually." Her Ladyship threw Mrs Spanner an icy stare but Mrs Spanner threw back an even dirtier one (one of her best!) and Her Ladyship turned to ascend the steps. "One-nil to me I finks," gloated Mrs Spanner.

"What the fuck you on about?" asked Kitty.

"Never you mind," said Mrs Spanner as she packed away the small cups and saucers.

"That wasn't nice, Mrs Spanner," said Phokker.

"Never said I was nice," sneered Mrs Spanner. "Give us a 'and getting the lunch table out, will ya, Phokker."

He did as he was asked and watched Her Ladyship swish her beautifully bustled backside slope up the steps and along the promenade until she was just out of sight.

His Lordship had been chatting to some chums that he'd known for many years, when he heard a familiar voice. "Hello, Dickie!" called Doctor Foster. "I didn't know you were coming here today?"

"Last minute idea, old chap," said Lord Dickie, "how's Sir Sidney this morning?"

"Not good, I'm afraid," answered the Doc, "will need to be kept in for further treatment." His Lordship winced as the Doc spilled the beans on what treatments had already been done to try and help with Sir Sidney's ailments. Electric shock treatment, immersive water treatments (a bit like ducking a witch in the old days, just not as prolonged) and the blancmange enema (everyone's worse nightmare!). It wasn't until Sir Sidney was threatened with a mackerel massage and wasp enema that he finally broke down and confessed to his wild outburst. He had been barred from attending his seat in the House of Lords a week previously, but he was still catching his early morning train, with his briefcase in hand, so he wouldn't have to tell his wife and bring shame upon himself and his family.

"What had he been barred for?" asked Lord Dickie.

"Well," started the Doc, "he passed a motion."

"And what's wrong with that?" asked Lord Dickie, "Happens all the time, doesn't it?"

"Ah, well, er…" paused the Doc, "It stank the whole place out and the carpet is still stained."

"HELLS BELLS!" exclaimed a shocked Lord Dickie. Fuckin' HELLS BELLS indeed!

Phokker helped the ladies set the table for luncheon, but seeing as that was easily nearly an hour away, Kitty decided to ask if she and Jack could go for a walk. "Don't be too long, as we'll be needed for luncheon soon," said Phokker, looking at his pocket watch.

Kitty squealed with delight, grabbed Jack's hand and dragged him along the sand. He looked nervous as he waved goodbye to Phokker. "And stay away from that bloody bandstand!" Mrs Spanner shouted after them. Kitty removed her shoes and stockings as soon as she was out of sight of Mrs

Spanner. She giggled as the sand enveloped her toes. She and Jack strolled along the shore line, picking up shells as they walked. She was fascinated by all the many shapes and colours of them and was in awe of Jack's knowledge about each one. She had no idea that tiny creatures had once lived inside of them.

"How'd they get in there?" she asked him.

"They grew inside of them," he answered. She didn't believe him at all and she slapped his arm.

"You're 'aving me on!" she laughed. Jack laughed along with her as their feet were swamped with foamy waves lapping gently on the shore. It was bloody freezing!

Her Ladyship was achieving admiring glances left, right and centre and she loved all the attention. She didn't give her husband a second thought as she waltzed along. He cared more about his new toy than he did her! Pillock! She meandered through the streets, then through some back lanes and into some dodgy looking alleys. A familiar odour filled her nostrils and her mouth suddenly became dry.

She sniffed the air to see if she could distinguish which particular brand it was, but there were too many delicious odours mixing together. "I have to find it!" she mumbled to herself. Just then, a small, bony finger came out from a dimly lit doorway and beckoned her. She sniffed the air once more and realised she'd found her prize. Above the door was a hand painted sign: GERTS GIN PALACE. She looked about and seeing as no one was around, she stepped eagerly inside. She handed her parasol and bonnet to a tiny lass at the door and parted the beaded curtain to reveal a palace of dreams. The dimly lit den was awash with the heady scent of a myriad of gins. The walls were filled with shelf upon shelf of gins from, what appeared, all over the globe! Her eyes darted furtively about, looking for that all too familiar label she loved the most.

"Can I help?" said a voice close by. Her Ladyship turned to find a statuesque woman, dressed from head to toe in brothel red. "The name's Gert; Gert Lush," came the introduction.

Gert was a well-travelled woman who had worked horizontally over most of the British Isles and beyond. Originally from Demport, Plymuff, she was led astray by her second husband, who was an ex-marine. She made him a pretty penny from working on her back, but he had far too many other girls working for him so she kicked him into touch!

After several other failed marriages, she finally decided that after husband number seven, she'd give up on men and all their constant demands to make them money from all her horizontal, acrobatic dancing. Plus, she was getting sick to the stomach of all the wedding cake! She found her little back alley bolthole in Saltbury by sheer accident…She'd fallen over a decomposing tom cat carcass and sprained her ankle. A huge tattooed chap, called Silas, picked her up and it was love at first sight. But marriage? Not a chance! Just plain old living in sin above her gin den would keep the wolves at bay and she had Silas to protect her. He didn't make any demands on her to make him money, which pleased Gert as all her orifices were getting well and truly worn out! Classy woman she was not, but this was her place and she was going to run it her way! Lady Khuntingham glanced at all the gin bottle adorning the walls and began to salivate.

"I'm looking for Dr Ginqu…" she started.

"Ginquakes Extra Ordinary Potato Gin," finished Gert.

"Why yes," said Her Ladyship, "do you have it?"

"Do I have it?" laughed Gert, "I got that and a shitload more besides!" Her Ladyship smiled and began to perspire. She needed a fix…just a small one.

"I'm…I'm…" said Her Ladyship, becoming dizzy.

"No need for names here, love," said Gert, "I'll just call ya Mary for now."

Lady Khuntingham grinned and glazed over. "I need to…well…not drink it," she said.

"Oh, serious shit!" said Gert. "Silas…get me the drip!" Her Ladyship had no idea what was going on as the stench of a thousand or more gins entered her nostrils and made her feel slightly queasy, but excited. As Gert led her Lady

47

Khuntingham along, Her Ladyship watched Gert's hourglass figure wiggle before her provocatively. Her red, strapless dress was slit up both sides which showed Gert's perfect pins and muscular thighs. Red skyscraper heels and a stack of bright, red, curly hair (obviously a wig…and a bad one at that!) topped her off. She was a sight for sore eyes. She was a sight for good eyes too! Her Ladyship thought that her dress had a strange pattern on its sleeve…but this dress had no sleeves. It was a tattoo! A long, red dragon's body and tail, wrapped itself around her right arm, with its tail ending on her middle digit. The mighty creature's head adorned her shoulders. Gert swished around and pointed to the corner. "Sit here," she said and sat Her Ladyship in a small booth, with seats covered in dark, purple velvet. "You'll be comfy here, Mary," said Gert. Silas approached with a stubby bottle of gin, rubber tubing and a deadly looking needle.

"What's that for?" asked Her Ladyship, confused.

"If you ain't drinking it, I'm guessing you're shooting it straight up your veins!" replied Gert. "Give us your arm!"

Lady Khuntingham, without a second thought, stretched her arm out onto the table.

"This'll hurt at first, but you'll soon be flying!" smiled Gert.

"Oh no she won't!" shouted Phokker from behind. "Get your fucking hands off her!"

"Get him Silas!" screeched Gert. Silas turned and Phokker stood face to face with the heavily tattooed thug, whose nose had been beaten out of shape so many times over the years, that it resembled the shape of a squashed, ripe tomato.

"I'll rip your fuckin' 'ead off if you don't get the fuck outta 'ere!" growled Silas. Phokker could see the distress in Her Ladyship's eyes as Gert grabbed at her and wrestled with her arm, trying to inject her with God only knows what type of cheap gin.

"She's a grown woman who can make her own mind up!" shouted Gert. But Phokker could see that Her Ladyship was far too dazed and confused to realise what Gert was trying to do.

"I'll count to free and you better leave…or else," Silas warned. Phokker stood and stared straight at him, unblinking. "One…two…" began Silas. "THREE!" yelled Phokker, and headbutted Silas with such force that he flew over the bar, scattering and breaking gin bottles as he did so.

The strong smell of mixed gin almost made Her Ladyship succumb, but Phokker grabbed the needle from Gert and pushed her to the floor. She produced a cutthroat razor concealed in her cleavage (what a place to keep a fucking razor!) and lashed out at Phokker's ankles.

"I don't think so!" shouted Her Ladyship, who kicked the razor from Gert's hand sending it flying into the air, plunging itself into the ceiling. Lady Khuntingham then kicked Gert violently in her nose, making her fall back, nose bleeding profusely. "There's a bit more red to add to your cheap, dirty look, you fucking whore!" screamed Her Ladyship.

Suddenly, Silas stood up and rubbed his sore, bulbous nose. "Is that all you got?" taunted Silas. Phokker ran at the bar and launched himself towards Silas. He cleared the bar easily and plunged the needle into the top of Silas', balding bonce. He sank like a sack of spuds.

"I don't know what was in that bottle," said Phokker, "But that was nearly in you!"

"Oh Phokker, you saved me!" Her Ladyship gushed. "Kiss me!"

"Let's get out of here before we get into any more trouble!" Phokker boomed and they ran through the beaded curtain. "My bonnet and parasol if you please!" snapped Her Ladyship to the tiny lass at the door. The young lass handed back Her Ladyship's belongings and ran inside to see if Gert was OK. "We shan't be back, you know!" bellowed Her Ladyship.

Phokker grabbed her hand and dragged her out into the alley, through the back lanes and out into the streets, where they met with the sunshine once more. "How did you know where I was?" she asked.

"I followed you," he replied.

"Why?" she inquired.

"Because I knew you'd get yourself into trouble being out on your own," he said.

"Thank you so much," she said and kissed his cheek.

"Not here, ma'am," he said, "Too many people about to see us. They'll only gossip."

"I'll reward you later then," she grinned wickedly and winked. His loins stretched his trousers to a maximum and his nethers ached for her, but here and now was not the place. He'd have her panting like a rabid panther back at the Abbey and ride her like there was no tomorrow!

Chapter Seven

Meanwhile, Kitty and Jack were still strolling along the shore, gathering shells and occasionally flicking the cold, salty water at each other. Neither had a care in the world and were enjoying each other's company. Suddenly, a melodic tinkling filled the air.

"It's the funfair," said Jack.

"Can we go?" begged Kitty, "Please?"

"Of course," said jack, "but you'll have to put your shoes back on."

Kitty sat on the sand and hoicked her skirt and petticoat up to her hips. Jack blushed as he'd never seen above a lady's knees before (and Kitty ain't no lady!). She dusted the sand from her feet and slowly pulled her stockings into place, tying each with a ribbon at the top. Kitty knew that Jack was watching and made an absolute meal out of the whole thing. She placed her shoes on and pointed a toe in his direction.

"Buckle me shoe up, Jack," she asked. Her skirt was right up high and Jack was able to see her pale pink bloomers as she placed her foot on his thigh. He blushed a shade of crimson that even Pantone hadn't made (or would even contemplate to make!), and he fumbled about with the fastening. His fingers forgot how to work and he had to look away to try and gain some composure.

He looked over at the rock pools. "Oh, look," he said, "crabs."

"I AIN'T GOT NO FUCKIN' CRABS!" shrieked Kitty, jumping to her feet.

"No, no, there in the rockpool," said Jack, but Kitty was insulted by his words and stormed off before poor Jack could explain himself. He followed her up the steps and watched as she paced through the crowds at the funfair, limping as she only had one shoe on. She bent down to put it on and Jack came up quick behind her.

"What the fuck do you want?" she hissed at him.

"The crabs were in the rockpool, silly," he replied.

"For fuck sake, why the fuck dint you say!" she barked.

"I tried but you wouldn't listen to me," he said. They stood silent, staring at one another, then laughed.

"Sorry," they said in unison and laughed again. All of a sudden, a loud, brash voice cut through the fairground chimes and the carnival folk.

"OY! KITTY!" it belted out from afar, but where? Kitty looked about and met the gaze of Salty Sal. Her sea-green eyes stared at Kitty viciously. Sal had her own whelk stall down the market and she was one (of many!) of the conquests of Freddie Drinkwater. Her golden hair danced in the breeze like a mermaid's, but she was far from one. As soon as she opened her gob, all illusions of her beauty were well and truly thrown out of the window. Originally from London, a right proper cockney she was, with a foul temper and fouler mouth.

Think Ray Winston (X10!), add in the sewer rat mouth of a merchant seaman, and you were almost there. Some say profanity was her middle name. But it was Ethel.

"What the fuck you doin' in my fuckin' neck of the woods?" Sal asked (very unkindly if you ask me!)

"I'm out with His Lord and Ladyship for the day," replied Kitty, "Besides, I dint realise I needed your permission!" Jack just stood gazing up at the squawking seagulls.

"You gonna tap up some fuckin' unlucky punter, are ya? asked Sal, "Or 'ave you brought that fuckin' twat, Freddie, with ya?" Freddie had bonked Kitty hundreds of times and had done quite a few rounds with Sal too. She was quite jealous of Kitty's magnificent chest, but Freddie also liked Sal for her saucy tricks with her whelks (gross!).

"Freddie Drinkwater!" scoffed Kitty, "You 'kin 'ave 'im!"

"'Ave him?!" Sal squealed.

"I got my Jack 'ere," said Kitty, dragging him to her side to show him off. Jack just smiled and waved. "'Andsome, ain't he," smirked Kitty.

"He's very clean," said Sal, "he wouldn't leave fuckin' sooty 'handprints on me aris!"

Kitty held Jack fast for fear of losing him to Sal, but she needn't be afraid as he only had eyes for her...and the circling, squawking seagulls.

Phokker and Her Ladyship walked along the promenade discussing how they could cover up her disappearance to her husband. They needn't have feared as he was still stood next to his motor vehicle, flicking through the brochure to tell all and sundry about it.

"See!" said Her Ladyship, pointing sternly towards her husband. "He didn't bloody miss me at all!"

"I'm sure he did," Phokker consoled.

"I'd be better off in that gin den with Gert!" she cried.

"You're not bloody going back there!" Phokker shouted.

"I've not heard you use profanity before," said Her Ladyship, "I quite like it; keep it up!" She gave him one of her saucy winks, knowing that his front trouser area would stretch out of his control. She was a wicked woman and she knew it: she loved it!

"Ah, there you are, me dear," Lord Dickie said, finally spotting her, "Did you have a nice stroll?"

She looked at her husband and was about to answer him, when a gentleman asked His Lordship if the motor vehicle came in another colour, apart from red. His Lordship's gaze drifted from his wife to answer the gent and she spun on her heels, storming off towards their spot on the beach. She was furious with him and decided to give the gin a go before he got his hands on it again.

"Before luncheon, ma'am?" quizzed Phokker.

"Hell fucking yes!" she replied and poured herself a rather large gin.

"You want tonic with that, ma'am?" asked Mrs Spanner.

"Hell fucking no!" she growled and she downed the gin in one huge gulp (what a great swallower!).

"What the 'ell happened to her?" whispered Mrs Spanner to Phokker, "And you for that matter?"

"I shall explain all later," replied Phokker, not trying to look the least bit bothered by all the stares that Her Ladyship was getting (Gentry never, ever poured themselves drinks outside their own home, so people seeing this were alarmed at her commonness and sneered down their noses at her).

"What the fuck are you all looking at?" she bellowed. They all looked away, slightly embarrassed, not by their actions, but of her foul language (Gentry used all sorts of language with their staff, but not with fellow toffs). Phokker became increasingly irritated by Her Ladyship's attitude towards others. He poured her another drink and came close to her ear. *Eau de Lapin* wafted up his nose.

"Stop this, or else," he whispered.

"Or else, WHAT?" she yelled back.

Mrs Spanner didn't know where to look, so busied herself rearranging the food in the wicker basket.

"Or else you'll get no more," he replied.

"I'll get my OWN bloody gin, thank you!" she scoffed.

"I mean, you'll get no more from me," bluffing her into submission, as he wanted to give it to her badly, but denying it from her would hopefully stop her tirade of abuse.

"You bastard!" she hissed, staring into his hazel eyes. Now she'd had him, she didn't want to lose him...Well, his massive willy anyway!

"You'd stop it?" she asked meekly.

"I most definitely would," he answered, knowing he didn't mean a single word of it.

"I'm sorry, everyone," she atoned and looked about, "I'm rather tired and in need of a lay down." She hoped her pathetic apology of tiredness would appease the other toffs and their staff. No one was interested.

"I really do need a lay down," she said to Phokker, "I do feel quite ill."

"I shall see if His Lordship will take us home," Phokker said.

"No, no," said Her Ladyship, grabbing at his forearm (I said forearm all right!), "I don't want to ruin his day out. I just need a rest."

"I shall see what I can do, ma'am," said Phokker and sat her back on to her chair.

He walked up and down the beach, chatting to other toff's staff and came back promptly with good news.

"Apparently, there are bathing huts for hire, ma'am," he said.

"But I don't want to bathe," she replied.

"But there is a bench inside," he explained, "where you can lay down and rest."

"That would be excellent, thank you, Phokker," she smiled. Phokker went in search of the man who hired out the bathing huts and was able to acquire one for an hour.

"Will that be a sufficient amount of time for a rest, ma'am?" he asked.

"Depends on if you'd like a 'rest' with me?" she winked.

"That may well prove impossible with all the people about, ma'am," Phokker said.

"I'm sure you'll think of a way," she smiled, "Now, where's this hut?"

Phokker took her a little way down the beach where a set of bathing huts stood next to the rockpools. He took the key from his waistcoat pocket and looked for number 11. It was right at the far end. He climbed the steps, unlocked the door and helped Her Ladyship ascend the wooden stairs.

"It's quite cosy in here," she said, brushing herself against his arm.

"It looks comfortable enough for a rest, ma'am," he replied.

"And more besides!" she winked with a wicked grin.

"Here is the key," said Phokker, balls aching, "I suggest you lock yourself in."

"Aren't you staying?" she asked.

"Best not," he answered, "not here." Phokker descended the steps and started to walk away.

"There's a back door, you know!" she called after him.

Phokker paused with his stiffened knob throbbing and turned slowly. "Keep it unlocked, I'll return in ten minutes."

Salty Sal was still giving Kitty grief over Freddie Drinkwater.

"Get over him," said Kitty, "I am."

Sal, not wanting to be outdone by a mere slutty housemaid, stood on her tiptoes and scanned about the funfair.

"OY! LAURIE!" she bellowed. "GET YA FUCKIN' ARIS OVER 'ERE!"

Kitty could see the crowds parting, but couldn't see anyone walking through them. Suddenly, a short, broad man wearing a red tartan kilt appeared before Sal. He was all of five-foot tall and built like a brick shit house for garden gnomes. Sal spun him around to face Kitty's direction.

"This 'ere is Laurie MacTavish," Sal said.

"Pleased to meet you, I'm sure," said Kitty, confused.

"This 'ere is MY bloke," Sal said smugly.

"Oh, right," Kitty smirked, stifling a giggle.

"He's a lobster man," said Sal, "ain't ya," giving Laurie a jab.

"Aye," came his reply in a deep, strong, Scottish accent.

"I wondered what the smell was," sneered Kitty (actually, only joking, as she'd lost her sense of smell if you recall).

"He's cleaner than that fuckin' Freddie!" scowled Sal.

"Don't you mind the smell?" asked Jack.

"What smell?" asked Sal, "I can't smell fuck all!" Sal was a smelly-arsed bitch herself, what with working with the whelks (try saying that when you're pissed!). "He loves me whelks," Sal said, jabbing Laurie again. Jack urged.

"Aye," came his reply once more.

"And I just fuckin' loves his lobsters, don't I," Sal said with yet another quick jab in his direction.

"Aye," he replied...again.

"He don't say much, do he?" quizzed Kitty.

"He don't need to say fuck all with this," said Sal, who promptly raised Laurie's kilt to reveal not only no underwear, but the fattest, longest shlong Kitty (or anyone else for that matter!) had ever laid eyes on...and she's seen quite a few in

56

her time! It looked like a veined salami hanging in a deli window. Talk about tossing the caber! Kitty's jaw gaped. Jack's jaw gaped. The funfair folk and all the people around gaped too. It was absolutely silent apart from the music coming from the carousel in the distance. Laurie stood there proudly, with both fists resting on his portly hips, while Sal smiled broadly at Kitty.

"How the fuck does that fit?" asked Kitty.

"Easy," said Sal, "with a little help from me whelks." Jack ran behind the coconut shy and puked his guts up. Even though he wasn't worldly wise, he got the gist of their conversation…but the whelks bit tipped him over to barfing point. Sal dropped Laurie's kilt, which just about covered his gigantic salami-like member.

"Let's leave these fuckers to it, shall we?" said Sal.

"Aye," answered Laurie and the mismatched sized pair waltzed off towards the bandstand. Kitty ran behind the coconut shy to rescue Jack.

"Are ya all right, Jack?" she asked.

"BBLLEURRGGHHH!" he heaved.

Kitty was really worried about Jack, but she needn't have been. The mere mention of whelks always had that effect on him. Bless.

Chapter Eight

Mrs Spanner, with the help of Dickens (who was the only one who hadn't deserted her) started to set the table for luncheon. Dickens' eyes watched Mrs Spanner's every move as she unloaded more and more delicious food from the wicker basket.

"Mmm, crumple 'ansum mmph tiz," drooled Dickens. Mrs Spanner just smiled, as she didn't have a bloody clue about what he'd just said. Where's Jack for translation when you need him, eh? Phokker returned to find them both very busy and capable of laying out the table between them.

"I shall go and find the others," he said to Mrs Spanner.

"Kin you start the primus off for us first?" she asked him. Phokker pumped the kerosene and lit it once more, placing the huge copper kettle on top. He then set off in the direction he came from and Mrs Spanner thought this rather odd, as Kitty and Jack hadn't gone that way. But she was well aware of who had gone there. "Bitch!" she mumbled under her breath.

"Whathefug?" said Dickens, aghast.

"Oh, don't mind me," she said, "'Ere, have a pork pie." Dickens' eyes lit up and he started to suck on the pastry. Gross.

Phokker walked around the back of the bathing huts and stopped behind number 11. He knocked thrice; slowly. The door opened and there he saw Her Ladyship's ankles waiting for him. "What took you so long?" she quizzed.

"I had to check how luncheon was going," he answered,

"We haven't got long as I'm meant to be looking for the others."

"Best you get in here then!" she replied. Phokker jumped up and climbed in, locking the door behind with a small, brass bolt. He spun around and dropped to his knees. His hands wandered over her shoes, brushing her ankles, caressing her calves and knees until he could feel the delicate, frilly edge of her bloomers. He placed his hands inside and ran them up and down her milky thighs. She shivered, moaned and panted, until she could take no more.

"I want you…NOW!" she screamed. Phokker yanked her bloomers down to her ankles and thrust his head up inside her skirt and many petticoats.

"Oh, my fucking Lord!" she shrilled, as Phokker's tongue danced all around her quim whiskers. His tallywhacker throbbed and as he released it, it bobbed up and down until he grabbed it and tugged at it hard.

"Turn round," he demanded, and she did as he bid. He held her hips and pulled her towards the floor, so she rested on all fours. Doggy style…nice! His todger was inside her slippery cup lightning fast and she gasped as his thrusting was long and hard. He reached around and fondled her breasts, releasing them from their corseted perch. The bathing hut was swaying and its wooden chassis creaked as it did so.

Phokker stiffened as he exploded and Her Ladyship shrieked too. Both were sweating, not just from their debauched activities, but it was bloody hot in there and the thought of them being caught made them anxious, but excited too. Her Ladyship went limp and his member slipped from her moist, pink pocket. Once again, he wiped it in one of her many petticoats and tucked it away. He stood up, and as he did so, raised her bloomers back into place. She was dazed so he lay her down on the little bench.

"I shall go and find the others now," he said. She simply smiled and waved. He unbolted the back door and slipped out, hopefully unnoticed.

Mrs Spanner had finished setting the table herself, as Dickens got into a lot of bother with the pork pie and lost another tooth. He was now left with one, solitary tooth, which jutted up from his bottom jaw like a crumbling, greying, tombstone. Mrs Spanner was wondering what was taking Phokker so long to find the others, when Jack and Kitty suddenly appeared.

"You on yer own?" asked Kitty.

"Well, I got Dickens 'ere, but he's no use now as he's gone and lost himself another bleedin' tooth!" said Mrs Spanner.

"Oh no!" Jack said and he walked over to comfort Dickens, who he could see was quite upset.

"Where's Phokker then?" asked Kitty.

"Looking fer you lot!" replied Mrs Spanner, surprised.

"Well, I'm 'ere now," said Kitty, "You want any 'elp?"

Mrs Spanner asked Kitty to set about making the tea, as His Lordship always liked a cuppa before his luncheon. Phokker and His Lordship came down the steps and apologised for being late.

"That's all right, Yer Lordship," curtsied Mrs Spanner, "Ta'int gonna get cold." Pork pies, gala pies, scotch eggs, cucumber sandwiches and even a jelly (which was quite close to collapsing from its dome-like shape) were set on the table before them. What a feast indeed! His Lordship licked his lips and Phokker sat him at the table.

"Where's the wife?" Lord Dickie asked, looking about.

"She was feeling a little unwell, sir," said Phokker, "So she went for a lay down in one of the bathing huts."

"Go and see if she's all right, old chap," said Lord Dickie. Phokker nodded and did as he was asked. This time, however, he knocked at the front door of the bathing hut. Her Ladyship peered out of the tiny window in the door, and upon seeing Phokker, she unlocked the door.

"His Lordship wants to know if you shall be joining him for luncheon, ma'am?" Phokker asked her.

"I may be able to take a spot of lunch," she replied.

"Your hour's up," said the bathing hut man, "and I won't breathe a word to anyone about your backdoor action!"

He winked in Phokker's direction, holding out his hand for a payment of some kind. Well, this was tantamount to blackmail for Phokker, so he grabbed the man by his throat and lifted him clear off the sand, dragging him around the side of the hut. He held the little scrote up against the wooden hut and the man let out a little, gruff yelp.

"Now listen to me, you piece of filth," snarled Phokker, "you are the lowest form of snivelling rat I've ever met!" Phokker's grip started to loosen, so he tightened it and raised the man higher. He let out another gruff yelp. "You saw nothing," said Phokker and he banged the man's head against the hut. "Do you hear me? Nothing!" The man nodded slightly as he started to turn a shade of purple. Phokker let him go and he fell in a crumpled heap at his feet. The man grasped at his sore neck, gasping for breath. Her Ladyship was in awe of Phokker's powerful grip and the way in which he had handled the awful man.

"That was magnificent!" she said, holding out her hand, "Please help me down the stairs." Phokker held out his huge hand and she clutched at it tightly to descend the steps. They walked off, leaving the near-choked-to-death man, still gasping for breath. He called out to his young assistant.

"Bring the pliers," he rasped.

"What for?" asked the young boy. The man rolled over on all fours and pointed at his bottom.

"To remove these fuckin' splinters!" he cried. Karma's great!

Luncheon was a rather quiet affair and Her Ladyship nibbled at it very little, but drank lots of tea, with copious amounts of gin on the side. His Lordship's appetite was as healthy as always and he'd slurped down half of the jelly before it completely collapsed. Phokker stood, like a sentry at his post, then cleaned away dishes and cutlery as, and when, they'd finished with them. Mrs Spanner and Kitty were able to wash them with the leftover water from the copper kettle, and then pack them back into the wicker basket.

"That was most delicious, Mrs Spanner," said Lord Dickie as he patted his rounded tummy.

"Yes, quite," added Her Ladyship, who had hardly touched a thing, as Mrs Spanner had noticed.

"Fancy another stroll, my dear?" His Lordship asked his wife.

"No thank you, dearest," she replied, "I'm still feeling a little wain." And she popped up her parasol to cover her face from the sun (I wonder how the face powder is holding up?).

"Well, I need to walk off some of this," said His Lordship as he patted his tummy once more. Her Ladyship waved him off, knowing that his stroll was only going to take him as far as his new toy. Hopefully he would tire of it soon, but she doubted it very much.

"Can you move my chair closer to the shore, Phokker?" she asked him.

"Of course, ma'am," he replied, and as she rose, he lifted her chair and followed her like an obedient puppy.

"Cow!" fumed Mrs Spanner.

"What the fuck you on about?" asked Kitty.

"Never you mind!" barked back Mrs Spanner, "Our time for grub now." Dickens' eyes lit up but he feared losing his one remaining tooth. "'Ere, 'ave the rest of this jelly," said Mrs Spanner, "That won't loosen anything!" Dickens' near gummy smile returned and he sat slurping jelly from the plate like a hoover. Kitty and Jack ate the leftover pork pie and saved the gala pie for Phokker, as it was his favourite. Mrs Spanner was quite glad of the rest and drank huge amounts of tea. No gin like Her Ladyship's gin. As Mrs Spanner always says, "Gin is a sin!"

Phokker returned and sat on the rough rug near Mrs Spanner. "What she up to then?" she asked Phokker, pointing towards Her Ladyship.

"Nothing," replied Phokker.

"I knows she got her eye on you," she said, "Be careful of that one."

"I have no idea what you are on about," Phokker said.

"Don't take me for a fool," she said, "I been watching the pair of thee." Phokker gulped his tea down and wiped the corner of his mouth with a napkin.

"There is nothing going on," he said, "nothing at all."

"Just don't be saying I didn't warn thee," she sneered.

Kitty giggled as she watched Queenie and Phokker sat closely together on the rug, with little knowledge of their serious conversation. "Them must be love birds like us," she laughed.

"I doubt it very much," scoffed Jack, "She's married."

"But Phokker ain't!" Kitty winked and elbowed Jack's ribs. Mrs Spanner heard the giggling behind her and had so far chosen to ignore it. She'd now had enough and turned to give Kitty one of her stares. Kitty soon stopped. "We're off for a walk now," said Kitty, "We'll leave you two alone." She grabbed Jack's hand and yanked him along the sand for fear of more scorn from Mrs Spanner.

"That girl's a cheeky bloody madam!" hissed Mrs Spanner.

"But she means no harm," said Phokker. They tided away the remaining dishes and shook the sand from the rugs, folding them neatly. Dickens was fast asleep, propped up against the sea wall, drooling and snoring loudly.

"Look at the state 'o' that!" moaned Mrs Spanner.

"Let him sleep," said Phokker, "Poor chap obviously needs the rest." They packed away everything, apart from the one chair that Her Ladyship was occupying. She was still sat looking out onto the glistening waves, watching them crash and break gently. Her eyelids became heavy and she drifted off to the sound of the water lapping at the shore.

His Lordship was, as Her Ladyship had assumed rightly, up at his motor vehicle, chatting to all the gents who were interested in his new mechanical wonder. He was most proud of it and enjoyed all the attention and adulation that came with it. Suddenly, there came a scream from the beach and Phokker knew exactly who it belonged to – Her Ladyship. Had that bastard bathing hire hut man come back to try his luck at blackmail once more? Phokker ran down to find Her Ladyship, quite alone, shrieking as her shoes had got wet from the incoming tide. Silly cow!

"My stockings are wet too!" she cried.

"They'll dry off," said Phokker.

"I want to go home!" she yelled, "I want to go home now!" He walked her up to His Lordship's car and sat her in the back. His Lordship didn't even notice that they were there as his head was under the bonnet to show off all the cylinders within (He had no idea what they did, but he'd sort of read about them in the booklet!).

"Er, cough, cough," Phokker said as he tried to get His Lordship's attention. "Her Ladyship wants to go home, sir." Lord Dickie poked his head out from under the bonnet.

"Home? What? NOW!" quizzed His Lordship.

"I'm afraid so, sir," replied Phokker. "Her shoes and stockings have become wet with the incoming tide." His Lordship slammed the bonnet down and plonked himself in the front passenger seat.

"You can sit back there," grumbled Lord Dickie to Phokker, pointing backwards with his thumb, "I'm bloody not!" Phokker could see that His Lordship was quite displeased with Her Ladyship. He returned to the beach, woke Dickens, and they, along with Mrs Spanner, carried the wicker baskets back up to the car. Dickens set off with the biggest one towards the horse and cart at the other end of the esplanade, with Mrs Spanner.

"You better go find Jack and Kitty," she called back.

"Where are they?" he shouted. Mrs Spanner pointed over the railings, towards the Punch and Judy show. Phokker called out to them both, but he couldn't be heard over Mr Punch's shouting,

"That's the way to do it!" As he beat the (un)living shit out of Judy. Phokker walked down and prodded them both in the back.

"We are returning to the estate now," said Phokker.

"What the fuck?" shouted Kitty.

"Less of your cheek," scowled Phokker and he started to march Jack back to the car.

"Look what I won at the fair," said Jack, holding up his prize in a small jam jar. But Phokker wasn't interested.

"Kitty, I suggest you catch up with Mrs Spanner and Dickens," called Phokker, pointing to the other end of the beach. Jack turned and gave Kitty his bounty to look after, as he had nowhere to put it while he was driving. Kitty was WELL pissed off at having to leave so soon. She'd had a lovely time with Jack.

As she skulked off to join the others, she couldn't help but wonder how Salty Sal fitted Laurie's enormous sausage in her hole. Mmm, me too!

Chapter Nine

Kitty was now the one with a face like a sulky, sour-arsed badger as the horse and cart slowly trundled its way back to the Ginton estate. Mrs Spanner, on the other hand, was positively radiant. Or at least as happy as a woman with a dead pike-slapped face could be. Dickens was still upset at the loss of his tooth and wondered if the Tooth Fairy would visit in the night if he put his rotten old tooth under his straw pillow. I can assure you that the Tooth Fairy wouldn't touch the greying monolith if it was the last tooth on Earth. She isn't that desperate! He tries a gummy whistle but all he produced was a stream of drool, which he wiped with his sleeve. It quickly became wet. Mrs Spanner was enjoying the ride and told Kitty to cheer up. "Why the fuck should I?" Kitty bit back.

"Coz we're goin' 'ome," replied Mrs Spanner.

"But I was really enjoying meself," Kitty sighed, "until that stupid bitch got her fuckin' shoes wet!"

"She fell asleep and the tide crept up on 'er," said Mrs Spanner, "T'aint her fault."

"Shouldn't sit so close to the fuckin' water!" Kitty growled.

Mrs Spanner could see that Kitty was furious with Her Ladyship and decided to stop trying to cheer her up. It was quite clear that she was in no mood to be talked with. "Remember to stop at the church," called Mrs Spanner to Dickens. "I got to collect me dues form the vicar."

His Lordship was becoming exceptionally jolly as the car chugged its way along and he waved at everyone, whether they were looking or not. Jack was growing ever more confident and accustomed to the car, so much so that his bum hadn't let out a nervous squeak for quite some time. This, as you may have gathered, was very good news, not just for him, but His Lordship's nostrils too! Her Ladyship had taken her shoes off and was moaning about her feet still being wet. Phokker suggested that she take her stockings off, but regretted it as soon as those words had left his lips.

"Oh Phokker," she exclaimed, "you are a naughty one!" And she hitched up her dress and petticoats, slowly and seductively, to pull her stockings down. "I may need a little help to remove them," she added saucily. Phokker was peering at her lily-white legs and pink ribbon edging on her bloomers. He became almost rampant and tried his very best to ignore her, but his trouser truncheon was having none of it. The material around his groin stretched so much that his scrotum became painful.

"You really must desist," he begged. She glanced at him, fluttering her eyelashes and pursing her rosebud lips. As she leaned towards him, he could make out a little bruising on her face.

"Is that bruise from last night?" he asked. She recoiled back into the corner of her seat and held her hand up to her face, trying to cover it.

"It's not that noticeable, is it?" she quizzed.

"Hardly," he replied, "you just came very close and I caught a glimpse; that's all." She removed a small powder case from her velvet purse and dabbed away at her face. "Here," said Phokker, "let me do it for you." She handed the powder case to him and he delicately patted around her eyes and nose, all the while trying to avoid her gaze, which he found entirely impossible. "There, all done I think," he said as he handed back the powder case. She checked herself in its little mirror and slipped it back into her purse.

"Thank you," she smiled, staring dead ahead, but she knew that Phokker was watching her pensively. And she loved it.

The horse and cart made its way back along the old road and Kitty was still in a foul mood. Mrs Spanner was eager to get to Piddleton and tried to hurry Dickens along.

"MMph Mozez ffphm crumple bumfp," moaned Dickens. Mrs Spanner didn't have a bloody clue what he'd said, so she sat back, knowing they were getting closer.

"What you gonna do to him this time?" Kitty asked sulkily.

"If he don't give me what I'm owed fer lookin' after 'is kids," scowled Mrs Spanner, "he'll be having his giggleberries for his dinner!"

"Can we try them?" asked Kitty, "I've not 'ad them before."

"You've 'ad far too many of them," replied Mrs Spanner, "and now you're on a strict diet!" Kitty looked confused. Dickens, who has been listening to their conversation, knew exactly what Mrs Spanner was on about, and he winced.

"MMph 'ere tiz Piddleton," he said. Mrs Spanner made out one single word that he said – Piddleton. She asked him to pull up outside the church. He got as close as he possibly could, as there was a carriage adorned with flowers, parked right next to the gate. She flew off the back of the cart and charged up the churchyard path in search of the vicar, checking the vestry first; empty. She knocked at the vicarage door and Franny, the vicar's wife, appeared at the door.

"I'm 'ere to see the vicar," Mrs Spanner hissed.

"He's not here," replied Franny, "He's in the church, but..." Mrs Spanner didn't wait for her to finish. She knew where he was and that was all she needed to know. She burst through the doorway thrusting the heavy wooden apart.

"OY, YOU! YES, YOU!" she bellowed, just as the vicar had asked,

"Is there anyone here today who knows why these two should not be wedded into holy matrimony?" The whole of the congregation turned to look at Mrs Spanner.

"Who the hell are you?" asked the bride, and the whole congregation turned their gaze to the front of the church. Mrs Spanner locked eyes with the vicar and he began to shake and sweat. "Well...who the hell is she?" the bride asked her groom.

"I've never seen her before!" he squeaked back.

"I'm 'ere for 'IM," growled Mrs Spanner, pointing straight at the vicar. The congregation turned to face the back.

"I don't know her," snivelled the groom, "Honest, I don't!" The congregation turned to face the front once again. The bride grabbed her groom's tie and squeezed it into a tiny knot until he choked.

"I'm afraid she's here to see me," said the vicar to the almost newly-weds. "Let me speak with her so she can be on her way." The bride took her hands from her soon-to-be husband's neck and crossed her arms. Her scornful look said it all. The vicar ran down the aisle, with his cassock flailing wildly. He grabbed at her elbow, trying to drag her from the church.

"Get yer 'ands off me!" she yelled.

"Please, don't make a scene," he begged (a bit late for that!), "Come to the vestry." They left and walked to the vestry in silence.

"You owes me an awful lot for them kids!" she barked at him.

"My wife knows nothing of this," said the vicar, "Can we keep it that way?"

"Depends on what yer offerin'?" she asked him. He removed a small key from under his cassock and unlocked a drawer in his desk.

"This is all I have," he murmured and produced a brown leather pouch about the size of a cricket ball.

"Is that all you got?" she scoffed.

"Please look inside," he begged, handing the pouch over. She opened the pouch and looked inside. It was full of gold guineas.

"What the 'ell are these!" she yelled, "How much is there?"

"There's a hundred guineas in there," replied the vicar, "Take them to the bank and they'll tell you you're a rich woman." She took the pouch and went to leave, pausing at the door.

"If it turns out that these are worthless," she hissed, "I'll be back."

"Oh, good Lord, please don't come back!" he begged, clutching at his still aching groin. Her finger stabbed at the air and she left. The vicar fell to his knees and thought himself extremely lucky that his family jewels were still intact. They still hadn't recovered from their earlier interaction.

The car chugged along Wigton Way and they were well ahead of the horse and cart. His Lordship was still smiling and waving at everyone they passed; many were unimpressed.

He saw a familiar sight drawing closer and he asked Jack to stop the car. He stood and waved at the oncoming vehicle, which stopped right next to his, totally blocking the road. "Hello, your Lordship," said Harry Strumpshaw, "How are you finding your marvellous new machine?"

"It's a real head turner," replied Lord Dickie, "Everyone stares."

"And how about you Jack?" he asked, "How are you finding the driving?"

"I'm getting more and more used to it," replied Jack, not daring to add that he'd shit his shorts the first time and had had constant bum squeaking moments since then.

"Where are you going with that fine-looking motor vehicle?" asked Lord Dickie.

"Oh, this was ordered months ago by Sir Sidney Squirrel," Harry replied.

"I'm not sure the poor chap's in a fit state to drive it at the moment," Lord Dickie said.

"Is he drunk again?" asked Harry.

"No, no, just a little unwell," replied His Lordship.

"He'll be as right as rain when he sees this!" said Harry.

"I do hope so," Lord Dickie said, "but he's not at home at the moment."

"Has he gone out?" asked Harry, "I sent a telegram to say it would be arriving today."

"He's having a spell in hospital," replied Lord Dickie, diplomatically.

"Well, it's paid for, so I'll leave it with his butler, Robertson," said Harry, "Cheerio!"

"Bye," shouted Lord Dickie as he waved Harry off. A massive trail of horses with carts on either side of the road had amassed, but no one had dared to shout at the gentry to move their bloody arses out of the way…flogging offence back then! Jack put the car into gear and off they chugged once more.

Her Ladyship had had her feet running up and down Phokker's legs all the while her husband stood there chatting to Harry. Phokker wanted to bang her one something awful, but had to sit there stony faced so not to give the game away. Now that the car was getting ever closer to the estate, His Lordship was feeling happier and chatted with Jack, unaware of what his wife was up to in the back. "You'll need to put your stockings on soon," said Phokker. She picked them up from the floor to find that they were still damp. She rolled them up into a ball and placed them inside Phokker's jacket pocket.

"Keep them as a memento," she purred. He was thinking that he'd rather have a pair of her drawers to tug himself off with later, but this was close enough.

"Thank you," he smiled.

She slipped her shoes back on and sat back in her seat, waiting for him to say something or to make a move; he didn't. She began to feel a little frustrated that the game she was playing wasn't going her way. Suddenly the car swerved as Jack's mother sprang out in to the road to wave at them and Her Ladyship was flung across the back of the car. She landed in Phokker's lap, with her bosoms right in his face. He didn't push her off though, as they were warm, comforting and smelt delicious. "Good catch, old boy!" cried Lord Dickie as he looked back to see how they were. Her Ladyship quickly climbed from Phokker's lap, after feeling his huge stiffy through her many petticoats. Jack was furious with his mother, as her stupid stunt had made his bum squeak to almost shitting his shorts, but not quite. The smell was unbearable.

"Is that my car?" quizzed Lord Dickie, sniffing the air.

"No, sir, I'm afraid that's me," said Jack.

"Oh…right," said His Lordship, who then asked Jack to have a word with his mother about endangering all their lives. He walked over to her and she could tell that he was annoyed with her. His face said it all.

"What the hell are you up to?" growled jack, out of ear shot of His Lordship.

"I been waiting for you to return," said his mum, "I got some of your things together for you to take."

"What?" Jack questioned.

"I found me another lodger," his mum replied.

"You found another lodger?" quizzed Jack in a state of shock, "In the time it took us to go to the seaside and back?"

"Well…yeah," she replied.

"No love lost there then!" Jack fumed.

"But fink of your ol' mum without your money coming in, Jack," she begged.

"But you ain't got to feed me no more!" he said crossly.

"I needs the money though, Jack," she moaned. Jack just couldn't make his mother see any sense and he was so shocked that she'd gone out and found herself another lodger so quickly.

"I'm off," he said.

"Don't you want any of your stuff?" she asked.

"I've no room on or in the car," replied Jack, "I'll collect it tomorrow." Jack jumped back into the car and realised it had stopped. He got out and was so furious; he jolted the car into life with one swift turn of the starting handle, without realising just what he'd accomplished. He put the car into gear and it jostled around the corner of Churchway towards the estate. They would soon be home and Phokker couldn't wait to get inside Her Ladyship's bloomers…again.

Chapter Ten

Mrs Spanner was looking forward to getting back to her kitchen. Kitty, on the other hand, couldn't give a shit as she sat with her sullen face on the back of the cart. She was plotting what she could do to upset Her Ladyship that evening, as she'd fucked up her day at the seaside with Jack. A happy bunny she was NOT. More like bunny boiler! "I'll fuck that bitch up!" Kitty mumbles to herself.

"I heard that, my girl," snapped Mrs Spanner, "Told you it weren't 'er fault." Kitty was having none of it though. She'd pay her back somehow. Dickens was approaching the corner of Churchway when, all of a sudden, Jack's mother came bounding out in front of them, waving frantically.

"Whatthefug?!" Dickens shouted, as the cart lurched forward. Mrs Spanner and Kitty held fast to the wicker basket to stop them falling out.

"What the fuck you up to Mrs P?" screeched Kitty. "You nearly made us crash!" Mrs Proudfoot went to the back of the cart and looked inside.

"You've enough room in there for Jack's stuff I'm guessing," she said to the pair and went to her gate to pick up his things. His old army kit bag, a tatty old suitcase and a beer crate. She loaded them onto the cart and walked away.

"What's all this?" asked Mrs Spanner.

"Them's Jack's things," she replied, "He was gonna pick um up tomorrow, but me new lodger needs the space."

"Another lodger? Already?" asked Kitty.

"I needs the money," said Jack's mother, "and he seems happy up at the big 'ouse with you lot."

"He's been with us less than a day!" snorted Mrs Spanner.

"Yeah, well, settled in," replied Jack's mother and she went indoors.

"The fuckin' ol' cow!" Kitty barked.

"Let's get on 'ome, Dickens," Mrs Spanner said, fuming at Jack's mother's barefaced cheek. Dickens cracked the reins and Moses plodded around Churchway. As they passed The Penny Whistle Arms, Kitty thought she saw a familiar face staring out blankly from an upstairs window. However, in the blink of an eye it was gone again.

Phokker jumped out of the back of the car as soon as it pulled up outside the Abbey. His Lordship waited for the door to be opened, but Phokker knew his place and let Her Ladyship out first. He then opened the door for His Lordship and promptly ran up the stairs to unlock the main door. "I'd like tea in the drawing room," she said to Phokker

"As soon as Mrs Spanner returns, I shall get her to do so," he replied.

"Must I wait?" she snapped, "Do you not know how to boil a kettle?"

Phokker was wondering where the nasty tone in Her Ladyship's voice had come from all of a sudden. He daren't ask her in front of His Lordship. "I shall go and do that now," replied Phokker and he watched her swish her way into the drawing room with Lord Dickie. He took the back stairs down to the kitchen and unlocked the back door. Jack stood there looking very pleased with himself, grinning broadly.

"I parked the car in the woodshed without crashing it!" he smiled.

"Well done, Jack," said Phokker, "Now help me with making tea."

"But that's woman's work!" Jack scoffed.

"Mrs Spanner isn't here and Her Ladyship's insisting on tea," explained Phokker.

"She can make it herself if she's that desperate," said Jack. Phokker stared hard at Jack, unable to believe what he'd just heard.

"Do you not know your place in this house?" Phokker snarled, with his temple throbbing.

"I…I…just…" Jack stumbled over his words.

"You are, along with the rest of us, lower than pond scum in the scheme of things around here," Phokker growled, "and don't you forget it!"

"Sorry," mumbled Jack, with his head down low.

He picked up the huge copper kettle and filled it while Phokker poked the range. The embers from this morning were still hot, so a prod and a little more coal brought the fire back to life. Phokker couldn't wait to poke and prod at Her Ladyship's bits, but why was she being so off when she returned home? He hoped that her fire hadn't gone out as he wasn't sure how or if he could rekindle the passionate flames within her. He'd had a taste of her after such a long wait. Could the flame have died as quickly as it had been lit? He hoped not or her hanky and stockings were the only things that would be getting anywhere near his throbbing loins.

Mrs Spanner didn't wait for the cart to come to a complete stop before she got off. She raced into the kitchen and gave the copper kettle a hug. "Fuck me, that's hot!" she shrieked, with a singed cheek and hands.

"Her upstairs wants a cuppa tea now," whispered Jack, "She told Phokker to do it."

"But that's MY job!" she demanded.

"I know, I told Phokker that," said Jack, "but I got a right earful for saying so." Mrs Spanner tutted and hung her coat up in the cupboard before wrapping her comfort blanket of a pinny around her thick waist and set to work. The teapot was warmed and the crocks were laid out on a tray in no time.

Phokker returned from the cellar to find all back to normal in the kitchen. "I shall take the tray up now," he said to Mrs Spanner, "Best you make a start on this evening's dinner." And he whizzed upstairs.

"I could do with a cuppa tea, Queenie," said Kitty as she strolled into the kitchen.

"Just a quick one, then set to work, my girl," said Mrs Spanner. She put Jack on spud-peeling duty and got Dickens to put all the wicker baskets from the car and the cart into the cellar.

"Whadda mmph baggins grumph, Jack?" asked Dickens.

"Why have you got my things?" Jack asked, "I was going to collect them tomorrow." Mrs Spanner explained that his mother had leapt out on them and nearly caused a crash. That she dumped all his things on the back of the cart and buggered off indoors.

"I can't believe it," said Jack, "She really has moved another lodger in already."

"Well, it's done now," said Kitty, "You lives 'ere wiv us now." And she smiled sweetly at him. Jack hadn't noticed her smile like that before now, and he liked what he saw. Her rosy cheeks glowed and her soft eyes sparkled in the light. Suddenly, he felt a strange stirring in his shorts. Something that had never happened before.

"I need the toilet," he squeaked and he ran to the outside block in the courtyard.

He fumbled with his trouser buttons, and as soon as he'd lowered them, his 'do-dah' (as his mother called it) was standing to attention, almost looking him in the eye. "What the fuck is happening?" he murmured. He wondered how the hell it would fit back into his trousers without drawing attention to himself. This poor unworldly lad was having his first stiffy and he had no idea what to do with it! As he tugged it this way and that, trying his best to fit it back into his shorts and trousers, a wonderful sensation ran through his whole body until one side of the brick shit house was redecorated white. "Where the hell did that come from?" he yelped. Upon looking down, he saw his 'do-dah' slowly returning to normal. "What a relief," he said, "I hope that don't happen again!" Thick twat!

Phokker had served the tea but was totally being ignored by Her Ladyship. He so wanted to pick her up and give her a right seeing to. However, he refrained from doing so as Lord Dickie would have given him his marching orders on the spot!

"Is the post in my study?" asked Lord Dickie.

"It is, sir," replied Phokker, "along with today's paper."

"I'm off to read my mail, my dear," Lord Dickie said to his wife. She merely smiled and sipped her tea. No sooner as

His Lordship left the room, Phokker stood next to Her Ladyship. His meaty thigh was pressed against her shoulder.

"What are you up to?" she asked him.

"I'd like to say the same!" Phokker replied.

"You seem to have forgotten your position around here," she grinned.

"What position would you like, ma'am?" he asked as he stood behind her chair. She leant back in her chair and could feel his groin against the back of her head. He pulled away and stood next to the fireplace.

"Why so cold towards me?" she asked.

"ME, COLD!" he stormed, "You're the cold one!"

"I have given you my best," she said.

"You spoke to me like…like…sh…dirt!" he snapped.

"SHIT! Go on, say it!" she hissed.

"SHIT!" he shouted.

"Oh, I love that filthy mouth of yours, Phokker," she said and raised her skirt and petticoats to show her bloomers and milky thighs. Phokker picked up the tea tray and left the room. Lady Khuntingham was aghast. Phokker was furious with her playing games. Normally he'd have shagged the arse off her something rotten, but being a complete bitch was not a turn on for him at all. He'd now play her games and keep her stewing for a while. See how the fuck she liked it!

Dinner was almost ready and Mrs Spanner decided that enough was enough…fresh gravy it was. She asked Kitty to take the old gravy pot and scrape it onto the compost heap.

"Not bloody likely!" she yelled, "I wrestled with that last time, plus you nearly blinded me wiv it!"

She asked Jack to chuck the gravy out. "Can do, Mrs S," said Jack.

"You'll need this," said Kitty, holding up a hammer and chisel.

"Cheeky cow!" screeched Mrs Spanner, "A spoon will do." Jack took the pot to the compost heap. He could still smell his shitty shorts from yesterday, festering away. As he scraped the weird looking gravy from the pot, he heard a noise behind him. He turned, but no one was there. As he loosened the last lumps from the bottom of the pot, he heard the noise again.

"Is that you, Kitty? Is anyone there?" he called out. A strange scratching, as if someone were digging their way out of their own coffin, could be heard. "Y… you…you…d…don't…scare…m…m…me!" he shouted. Suddenly, a little pair of beady eyes, glowing in the dim light, caught his eye. He swung the pot around and hit whatever it was with a mighty thwack. "That'll sort you out!" he yelled and he ran back to the kitchen with his arse omitting foul farts as he went! He burst through the kitchen door and told both women about his encounter.

"It's probably one of Dickens' chickens, you fool!" scoffed Mrs Spanner.

"Don't you believe in ghosts?" asked Kitty.

"No, I don't!" snapped Mrs Spanner.

She rang the bell for the lazy butler and Phokker pulled the first course skywards.

Chapter Eleven

Phokker served His Lord and Ladyship with the best butlering that you could have ever imagined. Etiquette? Check. Politeness? Check, check. Service? Check, check, check! No conversation, just simple and quick. Her Ladyship seethed at Phokker and he knew it. If she wanted to play games, then so be it! His Lordship chatted to his wife about Sir Sidney's treatment at the sanatorium, but she wasn't listening at all. His Lordship was used to this, so he continued to witter on anyway.

"I could do with getting out of this suit, Phokker," said Lord Dickie.

"Shall I put out your evening attire, sir?" enquired Phokker.

"I'll have my smoking jacket, if you don't mind," His Lordship replied, "No need to look like an old penguin when we've no guests this evening." Lady Khuntingham grew weary of their drab conversation.

"I'm going to retire to my room," she sniffed.

"But it's not even eight o'clock!" His Lordship scoffed.

"I'm awfully tired and need to lie down," she answered, sashaying across the dining room towards her husband. She held out her hand to be kissed by him. "Shall I expect a visit from you this evening?" she asked, but look directly at Phokker. He turned away, fuming, and slammed the cutlery drawer on the cabinet so hard that it sang a familiar tune. She grinned and knew that she'd got to him.

"I shall, if you so wish me to, my dearest," smiled Lord Dickie.

"If I'm asleep, just carry on without me," she smiled back, running her hand across the top of his balding bonce. Phokker knew what she was up to and so wanted to bite back at her, but now was neither the time nor the place. That would come; and so would he.

Mrs Spanner unloaded the crocks from the lazy butler and placed them into the foaming sink. Kitty started to wash them up just as Jack entered the kitchen. "Give us an 'and wipin' up, Jack?" she asked him. Her rosy cheeks, flush from the steaming sink, glistened in the lamp light and made Jack feel all 'funny' again.

"Oh shit," he mumbled.

"Is anything wrong, Jack?" Mrs Spanner asked.

"No, no, I'm, er, all right," he said uncomfortably. He faced the draining board and started to wipe the soapy plates. As he reached up to put them into the rack, his knob rubbed against the side. "Oooooohooooo," he muttered. Kitty just stared at him. He continued to wipe and place the plates up onto the rack, but with the constant knob rubbing, he quickly decorated the inside of his shorts. "Will you excuse me?" he said and he ran upstairs to his room.

"What the fuck's wrong with him?" Kitty said, totally bemused.

"Not a bloody clue!" replied Mrs Spanner. Jack changed his shorts (again!) and met Phokker on the back stairs near the kitchen.

"Are you all right, Phokker?" Jack asked him.

"Not really," sighed Phokker.

"Can I help at all?" asked Jack.

"I don't think so," said Phokker, "I have to tend to this mess myself, but thank you for asking." (so polite, ain't he!)

"What mess?" Jack quizzed him.

"Not to worry," replied Phokker, feeling slightly flustered by Jack's questioning. "Anyway, how are you?"

"Well, now that you ask..." replied Jack, who went on to explain what had happened to him when he looked at Kitty and his redecorating of the brick shithouse wall and his sticky shorts.

"That's all perfectly natural," explained Phokker, knowing that the attention was now well and truly off of him with the change of subject.

"That's not natural!" Jack squeaked. Phokker tried to explain all about the birds and the bees to Jack, but that only seemed to confuse him even more. So, he laid it out in simple laymen terms. "But that's DISGUSTING!" Jack shouted.

"Not when you feel that way about someone special," sighed Phokker.

"What are you talking about?" came a shout from Kitty, as the kitchen door swung open. Jack closed his eyes so he couldn't see Kitty's face.

"You have to control yourself, Jack," Phokker whispered in his ear. "You can't close your eyes forever." Jack slowly opened his eyes and he peered at Kitty. His groin twitched wildly, so he walked to the table and sat down to hide his shame. "A cup of tea all round, Mrs Spanner, if you please," Phokker asked. Kitty carried on washing the cutlery and Phokker sat with Jack. He quietly explained that there was no shame in feeling the way he did, hoping that this would put him at ease. He just had to have more self-control, or he'd run out of shorts in hours!

Her Ladyship was restless as she sprawled on the chaise. She was cross with herself as her powers of prowess seemed to be failing with Phokker. Little did the self-absorbed cow realise that by being a complete and utter bitch, she was going to get nowhere. She thought that the old 'treat um mean, keep um keen' was going to work. How very wrong she was. She rang the bell for Kitty to come and assist her undress, and when she arrived, she was very short with Kitty. "What took you so long?" she snapped.

"I was doin' the dishes," Kitty replied.

"Well, help me out of this gown," Her Ladyship insisted. Kitty did as she was told and placed the gown back into the wardrobe. Kitty also added a little something extra, pushing it way back in the wardrobe – left-over breakfast kippers. Revenge would be sweet for Kitty, but fishy as fuck for Her Ladyship.

"Is that all you be wanting?" Kitty asked.

"That's all," replied Her Ladyship, "for now." Kitty so wanted to punch her in her already bruised hooter, but knew that would mean the end of her working and living on the estate. Kippers would do…for now.

Jack was still in a state of confusion over what was happening to him and wondered if his life would ever be the same again. His bloody mother had a lot to answer for, as she'd made him live such a sheltered life, before and after his army career. Phokker's advice of slow breathing and focusing on something else should help him.

"What should I focus on?" asked Jack.

"Something simple," replied Phokker.

"Like Dickens?" Jack asked.

"Oh, dear Lord no!" reeled Phokker, "You'd never get a rise in your shorts ever again if you thought of him!" Kitty returned to the kitchen and smiled at Jack.

He smiled back and slowed his breathing, trying his best to focus on something else. His eyes glazed over. "It's worked Phokker!" he said.

"What did you think of?" enquired Phokker.

"Mrs Spanner's gravy!" replied Jack.

"What was that about my gravy?" Mrs Spanner demanded.

"Oh, nothing at all," Phokker said.

"Don't be talking about my gravy," she grumbled, "or you'll get what I gave Kitty yesterday!" Jack and Phokker looked at Kitty questioningly.

"She blinded me in both me eyes," Kitty explained.

"One time wif her gravy and the uver wif her fist."

"Mrs Spanner!" Phokker was shocked, "You can't attack staff over something as simple as gravy!"

"Now you see why I thought of it!" smiled Jack. Mrs Spanner cracked the back of Jack's head with the gravy ladle. "FUCK ME, THAT HURT!" he yelped.

"Just be glad there ain't no gravy on it, said Kitty. Mrs Spanner threw the ladle across the room but Kitty ducked just in time. It did, however, hit the plate rack with such violence that the whole rack came crashing down.

"Now look what you made me do!" screamed Mrs Spanner.

"ENOUGH!" Phokker bellowed. They all stopped and stared at him, mouths gaping like fish.

"You all need to work together and clean this mess up," he said. "Stop bickering and tidy up…NOW!"

Not a word passed their lips as they picked up the broken crocks from the draining board and the floor. Phokker got the large broom from the cupboard and started to sweep. The bell rang for the study. "That is His Lordship," said Phokker, "No arguing, just tidying!" and he left them to it. No sooner had he left the room, Mrs Spanner started again.

"T'aint nothing wrong with **my** gravy!" she insisted.

Phokker burst back into the kitchen. "I SAID ENOUGH!" he yelled, and promptly left again. As Mrs Spanner turned to sweep the crocks up from under the table, Kitty poked her tongue out at her.

"Saw that!" said Mrs Spanner.

"How the fuck?" Kitty squealed.

"HA! GOT YA!" Mrs Spanner shouted.

Jack thought he best step in and sort out the ladies. "Phokker said no more," he mumbled, "so please, no more."

"Sorry," said Kitty, rubbing his arm softly.

"I gotta think of something else now!" he said, as he decorated his shorts again! (another quick change required)

Phokker knocked at the study door but there was no reply. He knocked louder, but still nothing, so he walked in. There sat a fearful looking Lord Dickie as Sir Sidney Squirrel stood over him with a fireside poker at his throat. Phokker was alarmed, but didn't show it. Instead, he tried a diversion tactic (cool as an Eskimo's arse sitting on an iceberg!).

"How are you this evening, Sir Sidney?" Phokker asked politely. "Would you like a drink, sir?" For a brief moment, Sir Sidney dropped his guard to look at Phokker, but realised what he was up to. Lord Dickie wasn't quick enough to make a move from his chair though. Phokker went to the drinks cabinet and poured two glasses of port, then placed them onto a silver tray. He walked towards them with a plan, but Sir Sidney suddenly shifted position and stood behind His Lordship, poker now placed firmly under His Lordship's wobbly chins.

"Port for you both," said Phokker. "Th...th...thank...you," murmured His Lordship, and went to reach for a glass. Sir Sidney pulled back tightly on the poker, while Lord Dickie clutched at Sir Sidney's hands, with ill effect.

"You're hurting him, sir," said Phokker.

"AND?" yelled Sir Sidney.

"He's one of your oldest friends," explained Phokker, "Why do you want to hurt him?"

"WHY?" screeched Sir Sidney pulling back harder.

"Please put the poker down. He can't breathe," said Phokker, who was showing his anxiety. Lord Dickie was turning purple and he struggled to loosen the mighty grip holding him fast. Phokker picked up both glasses of port and downed them in succession.

"Please forgive me, sir," he said and he launched the silver tray, Frisbee style, at Sir Sidney's head. THWACK! It twatted him on the forehead and he sank like a dead weight in water, falling back into the long curtains. His Lordship gasped and spluttered as he crawled along the floor to escape his so-called friend's clutches. Phokker found Sir Sidney out for the count behind Lord Dickie's high-backed chair with a rather large indentation on his forehead.

"Is he all right, old chap?" asked His Lordship gruffly.

"I think so, sir," replied Phokker, "can you help me get him to the sofa?" They lay him down and Phokker poured His Lordship a large gin and tonic. He gulped it quickly, then shook the glass in Phokker's direction.

"Hold the tonic next time please!" Phokker poured him a neat gin and asked him to keep an eye on Sir Sidney while he fetched Jack. "What if he wakes?" asked Lord Dickie.

"Hit him with this," replied Phokker, passing over the coal shovel.

Lady Khuntingham smothered cold cream all over her face and gently massaged it in. Her nose was still quite sore and she knew that she'd have to cover up the bruises again tomorrow, especially for Sunday church service.

Kitty's earlier suggestion of using a big hat was now becoming a really good idea, but she needed one with the biggest brim she could possibly find. She reached up to the top of her wardrobe and took down as many hat boxes as she could. As she stepped from the chair, she thought she could smell something fishy.

"Fucking hell!" she retorted, "Is that me?" She lifted her dressing gown and wafted it about a bit as she bent over trying to sniff at her snatch. "Not me!" she said to herself as she continued to go through the hat boxes, looking for a whopper of a hat. It didn't take long to find one, but what did she have to match the huge purple titfer? As soon as she opened the wardrobe door, it became apparent as to where the smell was coming from. It was dark inside, so she had to fumble about a bit. "ARRGGGHHHH!" she screamed. "WHAT THE FUCK IS IT?" She had grabbed a handful of the bony fish carcasses and she quickly withdrew her hand from the wardrobe to find kippers in her grasp. "That fucking Kitty will pay dear for this!" she yelled and stormed down over the stairs towards her husband's study. She flung the door wide to find a sparked out Sir Sidney on the sofa, with her husband standing above him; gin in one hand, shovel in the other. "WHAT THE FUCK ARE YOU DOING?" she screeched. Before he could answer, Phokker and Jack came rushing into the study with some rope. Phokker stared at Her Ladyship in just her silky dressing gown with cold cream still on her face and a handful of breakfast kipper carcasses.

"WHAT THE HELL IS GOING ON?" they all shouted in unison. This startled Sir Sidney, who jumped so violently from the sofa, that he banged his head on the shovel and knocked himself out...again!

Chapter Twelve

Doctor Foster came as soon as he received the telephone call from Phokker. Nurse Boggins accompanied him just in case Sir Sidney required another sleeper hold to succumb him. Nurse Boggins was built like a Sherman tank and nobody messed with her...apart from Doctor Foster that is.

"How on earth did he get in?" asked the doctor.

"We've been to the seaside for most of the day," explained Phokker, "and I assure you that everything was locked up tight."

"Perhaps he waited until we returned?" said Jack.

"Mmm, that's possible," replied Lord Dickie.

Doctor Foster was amazed at how Sir Sidney had travelled so far with a broken leg. "He's taken his splint off," Doctor Foster said, pointing at Sir Sidney sparko on the sofa. Nurse Boggins promptly set about applying a new one. Lady Khuntingham sat in the fireside chair with a large gin (and no tonic), hiding her cold-cream-smothered face. Phokker discreetly handed her his handkerchief so she could remove it. As she did so, the bruises were clearly visible. Phokker pointed to his nose and raised his eyebrows at her. She panicked.

"I'm going to my room," she squeaked, and left without looking at anyone. She slammed the study door behind her and felt dizzy.

"I need a bloody drink...or something stronger!" she said, thinking of the locked ottoman at the end of her bed.

"I've no need to sedate him, so Nurse Boggins will put him in my carriage," said Doctor Foster.

"What if he wakes and attacks you?" asked Lord Dickie.

"Nurse Boggins will have no trouble handling him!" the doctor winked. She threw Sir Sidney over her shoulder and carried him with ease out to the waiting carriage. "Strong woman that!" said Doctor Foster, who winced in pain at his slightly singed todger, which Nurse Boggins had bandaged the night before. He clutched at his groin.

"Ah yes, dear boy. How is the old chap?" said Lord Dickie, pointing downwards.

"It'll get there slowly," he replied, "but when that woman does something like that, it gets me going and my bandage tightens."

"Oh, er, well, I do hope Sir Sidney gets better soon," said His Lordship, changing the subject.

"I'll have to lock him in his room from now on," said the doctor, who picked up his medical bag and shook His Lordship's hand.

"You mean he wasn't locked in?" exclaimed Lord Dickie.

"We try not to lock anyone in," said the doctor, "unless absolutely necessary."

"How did he slip out without detection?" asked Lord Dickie, "Isn't there an enormous, high wall around the sanatorium?"

"There is indeed," answered the doctor, "but he'd overpowered one of the male staff and stole their uniform coat…waltzed straight past the guard on the gate."

"With a broken leg?" Jack quizzed.

"Apparently so," mused the doctor, "Anyway, I'll keep you informed."

"Oh yes, please do," Lord Dickie said. Phokker and Jack walked the doctor to his carriage.

"I've got some rope here to tie him up," said Jack.

"I don't need rope when I've got Nurse Boggins about," grinned the doctor. As the carriage left, Phokker could have sworn he heard the doctor say, "Nurse Boggins, my bandage has become too tight again."

Lady Khuntingham was rifling through her dressing table drawer, trying to find the key to her ottoman. She was becoming more and more anxious and she scattered trinkets

87

and precious things about the floor in her search. Suddenly, she caught sight of the silken ribbon that was attached to the key and snatched it up. "There you are!" she squealed in delight. She dropped to her knees in front of the ottoman and fumbled with the lock. Her hands shook. She threw the lid open and discarded the itchy woollen blankets (yes, she still has them) and scrambled about in the bottom of the ottoman. Her prized (and very secret) gin box had disappeared.

"Where the fucking hell has that gone?" she snarled. And with that, she knew immediately of the one and only person who could've possibly have removed it. "Phokker! FUCKER!" she yelled. She was in a furious rage and threw hats, blankets, clothes, shoes and anything she could lay her hands on, across the room. Tears stung her cheeks as she rampaged about her boudoir. She suddenly caught sight of herself in her dressing table mirror. What a fucking mess! She fell to the floor and began to sob violently. What on Earth had she been thinking? She lay on the floor, for what seems like an age, feeling very sorry for herself. She knew deep down in her heart, that Phokker only had her best interests in mind, and that he'd saved her from God only knows what type of rotten, cheap gin fix earlier that day. She pulled herself up using the bedclothes and surveyed her room. "What have I done?" she whimpered. She went to ring the bell pull for Kitty's assistance in clearing it all away, but paused. "What would I say happened? Kitty would only tell everyone else," she muttered. She picked up the woollen blankets. "I really must get rid of those!" she said and locked the ottoman, placing the key at the back of her dressing table drawer. She then made a start at picking everything else up. Her room still reeked of kippers, so she raised the sash windows wide. She saw Phokker and Jack waving off Doctor Foster, so she waved at them, but they hadn't seen her.

Or so she thought. Phokker had seen her quite well enough and had every intention of paying her a visit later to give her a piece of his mind. Well, to give her something.

Lord Dickie was feeling rather peckish after his near-death poker experience. He often became hungry under pressure, I guess that's why he's a slightly portly sort of chap now! Not obese. No, no; just chubby.

"I'm famished!" he said to Phokker, as he and Jack returned to the study.

"I shall see what Mrs Spanner has for a light supper, sir," said Phokker.

"I'll go," quipped Jack, who skipped down over the stairs, raring to tell all to Kitty and Mrs Spanner about Sir Sidney's outburst.

"I'll get you another gin and tonic, sir," said Phokker.

"Without the tonic," pleaded Lord Dickie, who threw the gin back quicker than a snotty sniff. "Another please." And that went down with one gulp too.

"I think you better have something to eat, sir," said Phokker, concerned at all the neat gin consumption.

"I would if Jack shifted his arse!" replied His Lordship. Just as Phokker tugged on the bell pull, Jack appeared with ham, cheese, crusty bread and pickled onions. His Lordship held his hands out like a small child who wanted picking up, making grabbing motions with his hands.

"Mmmm, looks delicious!" Lord Dickie smiled.

"We shall leave you to your supper, sir," said Phokker, "but if there is anything else that you require, do not hesitate to ring the bell, sir." Phokker picked up the smelly kipper carcasses and wondered what on earth Her Ladyship was doing with them. Lord Dickie waved them off, stuffing a large pickled onion into his mouth.

"Er, remember to chew that, sir," said Phokker, "we don't want another *Hotel du Cheval* incident." His Lordship started to chew loudly and they left to have their own supper.

"What happened at Hotel du whatsit?" asked Jack. On their way down to the kitchen, Phokker told Jack all about an incident that happened a few years back. His Lord and Ladyship went travelling in Europe, staying at many fine hotels along the way. Phokker, obviously, travelled with them. Late one evening, His Lordship became hungry and insisted on having pickled onions. The staff in the hotel had no idea what Phokker was asking for. He even tried speaking to the kitchen staff, but no luck. He decided to go out and look in the local shops. He didn't have to go very far, but the shop was closed. Most owners lived above their shops, so Phokker banged away on *Café Cornichon's* door until someone appeared at the window. He flashed some francs about in the air and the owner soon came down. Phokker pointed at a jar of pickled onions in the window and francs and pickles were exchanged, all without a single word.

When he returned to the hotel, Lord Dickie was ecstatic. However, in his excitement, as he popped one into his mouth, he inhaled far too quickly and it became lodged in his throat. Lord Dickie clutched at his chubby neck, trying to gasp for air. Her Ladyship was completely useless and told her husband to stop messing about. He turned a nasty shade of blue and slumped to his knees. Phokker whacked him on the back, but it just wouldn't shift. He opened a window and bent His Lordship over the balcony, slapping his back frantically. Suddenly, with a mighty wallop, the onion dislodged and flew through the air. Fast. So fast in fact, that it twatted a gendarme riding past on his bicycle, knocking off his hat, which fell into a muddy puddle. "MERDE!" he shouted furiously. Phokker pulled His Lordship swiftly back into the room and slammed the window shut. He gave him a drink and snuck a peek from behind the curtains to see if the gendarme was still there. The gendarme stood, looking incredibly puzzled, with dripping wet hat in one hand and pickled onion in the other. He looked around and then looked up. He walked into the hotel reception. Phokker awaited a knock at the door, but nothing came. In the morning there was talk of what had occurred, all overheard while eating their breakfast in the dining area. They promptly left that same day and hadn't returned to France (or anywhere else in Europe for that matter!) since.

Her Ladyship had tidied away all of her hats and picked up most of the shoes that she'd thrown; or at least the ones she could find. Her room was becoming less pungent and while the window was still open, she decided to hang some of her gowns on the curtain rails to air them out. It was quite a stretch, even standing on the back of the chaise, but she managed to hang up a few. "I can't believe Kitty would stoop to doing such an awful thing," she grumbled (not a fucking conscious bone in her body that woman!). She sat at her dressing table and removed the hair pins, keeping some of her curls in place, one by one. Her soft curls unfurled and she gently ran her fingers through her locks; hair falling about her shoulders and brushing against her décolletage. She secretly wished that Phokker's huge, hairy hands would brush against that delicate area and fumble about to caress other soft, squidgy bits. With her eyes closed, she ran her fingers across her exposed shoulders and upper chest, imagining his rough touch. A shudder raced down her spine and a saucy smile passed over her lips. She breathed in deeply and the stench of old kippers caught her in the back of her throat, which brought her back to reality pretty damn quick! "I'll have to sleep with the window open now," she said, "I'll fucking freeze!"

"Do you know anything about these, Kitty?" asked Phokker, who was holding up the kipper carcasses in front of her.

"No," she squeaked as she reeled back from the stinky bones. She looked at the floor and picked at her pinny.

"I'm not sure I believe you," Phokker said. Kitty fumbled with her bonnet, but still didn't look up.

"I threw them out this morning," said Mrs Spanner, "Put them on the compost heap meself." Phokker waved them under Kitty's nose. She recoiled.

"All right, all right!" she shouted, "It were me!"

"Why?" Phokker demanded.

"What you been doing, my girl?" steamed Mrs Spanner.

"I put them in her wardrobe coz I fuckin' 'ates her!" Kitty screeched.

"What has she done to you to make you hate her so much?" asked Phokker.

"We had to come 'ome early coz of 'ER!" Kitty cried, "I wanted to stay at the seaside with…with…" Kitty sobbed loudly into her pinny.

"Me," Jack said sweetly. Kitty nodded and she ran into the courtyard. Mrs Spanner gave Jack a shove and told him to go after her. He was reluctant, but with a little gentle persuasion and a reminder to take it 'slow' from Phokker, he followed her outside.

"Put the kettle on, Mrs Spanner," asked Phokker, "I need a strong cup of tea."

Jack stood there like a total lemon as Kitty sobbed into her now quite damp pinny. Her shoulders heaved as her cries became more laboured.

"Are you all right?" Jack asked nervously. Kitty shook her head. He placed a trembling hand on her shoulder, not really knowing what to do in this situation. He'd never come across a sobbing woman before. Kitty turned and threw her arms around Jack's neck and nuzzled into his jacket collar. His whole body went stiff and he started to hyperventilate.

"Slow, slow," he could hear Phokker's voice in his head. He breathed slowly, over and over, which made his heart rate come back down and not want to jump out of his mouth.

"Hold me, Jack," said Kitty. Jack's arms felt almost stuck to his sides. "Please?" begged Kitty, "Just hold me." Jack loosened up and placed an arm around Kitty's slender waist, concentrating on his breathing as he did so. He placed his other arm around her shoulder and felt at ease with Kitty resting there. "Thank you, Jack," she whispered. Phokker came out into the courtyard and gave a little cough; just enough to make the pair realise that he was there, not to scare the shit out of them. Jack stepped back and straightened himself out.

"I think we'll go and see Her Ladyship now," said Phokker.

"Why do I need to see Her Ladyship? asked Jack (thick as shit, this lad!).

"Not you," said Phokker, rolling his eyes, "Kitty." Kitty looked at Phokker and gave no argument.

"Time to apologise, don't you think?" he said to her. Kitty just nodded in agreement and followed him indoors.

Chapter Thirteen

Jack was sat with Mrs Spanner drinking yet another hot brew. He took a huge swig and held it in his mouth, a sudden realisation hit him just like Mrs Spanner's ladle had done earlier. He gulped down the mouthful of tea loudly. "You all right, Jack?" asked Mrs Spanner.

"No...no, Mrs S," replied Jack, "I just realised something..." and he glazed over once again.

"What?" she quizzed, prodding him back to life.

"It must've been Sir Sidney that I hit in the garden earlier," he said, staring ahead.

"When you saw them beady eyes you mean?" she recalled.

"Yeeeahhhh," he said slowly, unblinking. "I didn't half whack him with your pot, you know!"

"Well don't be worrying 'bout that now," she said, "The doctor will look after 'im."

"I do hope he'll be OK," he mumbled with slight guilt, blinking for the first time in ages.

"E's in the best place for 'e, you knows," she said, smiling, trying to bring some comfort to Jack. "My uncle was in the very same place, you know, and that lovely Doctor Foster looked after 'im well."

"Really? How so?" he asked.

"Let's have another cuppa," she said and she went on to explain how her uncle was savaged by a blenny while rock pooling for crabs (the family were somewhat unlucky where fish and crustaceans were concerned!). They thought that he had rabies, what with all the mad foaming at the mouth, but a young doctor, fresh out of medical school, diagnosed ichthyospumaminordinationem and he was able to treat the symptoms with various pills, potions and suppositories in a variety of sizes. The most successful of all treatments was the attaching weights to his scrotum which gave him such excruciating pain, that he forgot all about his blenny attack. This, however, stretched his scrotum to knee dangling lengths and he required several new pairs of specially made medical trousers. He was slightly sedated overnight so that the weights could be detached in order to give him a little rest bite, but the nightmares were still there and he'd wake in a terrible sweat, lashing out at anything. They had to shackle him to his bed for his own safety. He was also unable to return home to his family for these reasons, although they would visit him, as would she. As the years rolled by, his children married and moved away. His wife would visit him once a month, until she too moved on with a travelling salesman from Didcot (who sold chastity belts for sheep – yeah, they weren't a great success!) "'E died at the ripe old age of 92," she said, wiping away a tear. "'Ee left me everything 'e 'ad."

"That was nice of him," said Jack.

"I still have them hanging in the cupboard," she said and opened the cupboard door to reveal two cast iron weights hanging on their chain to a rusty nail in the door. Jack crossed his legs, wincing.

"Can I have another cup of tea, please?" he asked.

Phokker went to knock on Her Ladyship's door but Kitty held onto his forearm to stop him. She gazed up at him with sorrowful eyes, which were welling up in the corners; her bottom lip all a tremble. But Phokker didn't fall for it. "You **will** apologise," he said to her sternly.

"Ah fuck it," she grumbled, "'Ow the fuck dint that work?"

"I've known you long enough and observed you many times using the same tactics on others," he replied, "So, it won't work with me." He then knocked at the door three times. Kitty sulked.

"Who is it?" Lady Khuntingham asked.

"It's Phokker, ma'am, came his reply. Her Ladyship dashed about the room nervously, as though a new bride awaited her husband's first lustings. She jumped up onto the bed and splayed herself out. She rolled onto her side facing the door, and pulled her dressing gown from her shoulders to reveal just enough cleavage for maximum impact on his bewitching, hazel eyes.

"Are you all right, ma'am?" he asked, after waiting ages.

"Just a minute," she answered, checking herself in her hand mirror. Gorgeous!

"I've got someone here who needs to apologise to you," he said through the door, knowing that she was probably in there preening herself for his entrance.

"What?" she squeaked, "I mean, who?"

"Kitty, ma'am," he replied.

"For fuck sake!" she muttered under her breath, "All that fucking faffing about for nothing!" She got off the bed and pulled her dressing gown around her tightly, tying up the silken belt, then sat at her dressing table and proceeded to comb through her locks. "Come in," she quaffed.

Phokker opened the door and gestured to Kitty to enter. She shook her head defiantly. Phokker placed his huge hand on her back and gave her a gentle shove into the room. She tried digging her heels in, but this just made her glide more easily over the Persian rug. Her Ladyship could see what was going on in the mirror but didn't turn.

"How can I help you?" Her Ladyship asked.

"Kitty has come to apologise, ma'am," he replied.

"I have…mmmmph," mumbled Kitty, then went to rage at Her Ladyship. Phokker placed his hand over her mouth.

"What do you need to apologise for?" asked Her Ladyship, knowing too well. Kitty bit down hard on Phokker's fingers, which he retracted quickly and she barged towards Her Ladyship.

"You knows what you fuckin' did!" Kitty shouted.

"Who on earth do you think you are?" Her Ladyship gasped.

"You ruined my day out!" Kitty screeched, tears now streaming down her hot, flushed cheeks.

"Me? Ruin **your** day!" asked Her Ladyship.

"Say sorry now," snarled Phokker, "and we will leave."

"NO!" yelled Kitty, "Not until I tells 'er!" Phokker went to grab Kitty to remove her from the room.

"Leave her, Phokker," Her Ladyship insisted, "Tell me what?"

"Just coz you got your bloody feet wet we 'ad to come 'ome!" sobbed Kitty, "I was having a lovely time with...with..." but Kitty's sobbing became so heavy that she couldn't draw breath and she crumple into a heap at Her Ladyship's feet. Her Ladyship looked up at Phokker and realised that she too would have to make an apology...for being such a bitch. She placed a hand on Kitty's shoulder, but said nothing.

"I'm sorry for putting them kippers in yer wardrobe," Kitty mumbled, "But it was me first time ever at the seaside. Her Ladyship felt a small pang of guilt.

"But kippers; really?" asked Her Ladyship.

"It was wrong of me, I knows that now," cried Kitty, "but me an' Jack was...was..." Kitty began to sob into her pinny again.

"I had no idea it was your first time at the seaside," Her Ladyship said, "Who's Jack?"

"His Lordship's new chauffer, ma'am," replied Phokker.

"Oh, the chap who drives his new toy!" she quipped, "Do you love him, Kitty?"

"I fink so," mumbled Kitty through her pinny.

"You only think so?" asked Her Ladyship. Kitty raised her head and her blotchy, red face broke into a smile.

"I knows I loves 'im," sighed Kitty, "'E's the only fella fer me from now on."

"How many have you had?" Her Ladyship asked, shocked.

"Too many to count, so Queenie says," answered Kitty.

"And who's Queenie?" she asked.

"That's Mrs Spanner, ma'am," replied Phokker, watching the woman of his dreams actually show some compassion for someone (anyone!) for possibly the first time in her life.

"So that's her name," Her Ladyship said, "I never knew."

"Only coz you don't ask," said Kitty.

"That's enough cheek, Kitty," Phokker said.

"No, let her go on," Her Ladyship insisted.

"I bet you don't know anyone's names who been through 'ere over the years," said Kitty.

"I know yours," Her Ladyship answered.

"Oh, all right, you knows mine," Kitty said, "But I don't even know if that's me real name."

"How could you not know your real name?" Her Ladyship asked. Phokker explained how Kitty was found by Dickens in the cabbage patch all those years ago, not able to do or say much. But with time (a bloody good bath!) and patience, she was nursed back to good health by Mrs Spanner and put into service. "I really had no idea about any of this," said Her Ladyship, "I'm so very sorry."

Kitty had never heard Her Ladyship say sorry and was surprised that the word was actually uttered by her at all.

"Why you sorry?" asked Kitty, "You dint know."

"But I should have made it my place to know," she replied. She gazed up at Phokker. "Does my husband know all of this?"

"I don't believe so, ma'am," he answered.

"Then I shall make sure he does," she replied, with all sincerity. She leaned forward and placed a finger under Kitty's pretty, little chin. "I'm so sorry," she repeated.

"And I'm sorry too," Kitty said, blowing her nose on her pinny. "I needs to make sure I gets the stink out of them dresses now!" She stood and tried to reach the gowns hanging on the curtain rail.

"Let me help you," said Her Ladyship, who stood on the back of the chaise, revealing her milking thighs as she did so. Phokker just stared.

"Are you gonna 'elp?" asked Kitty, "Or you just gonna stand there and gawp?" Her Ladyship turned to look at Phokker and saw an all too familiar bulge in his trousers. She smiled at him and his trousers twitching wildly about his groin. She took the gowns down and passed them to Kitty.

"I shall want to wear the purple one for church service tomorrow," said Her Ladyship, "If that's no trouble?"

"I'll get to work straight away!" said Kitty who left with an armful of rainbow-coloured garments.

"Would you help me down please?" she asked Phokker. He grabbed her tiny waist with his huge shovel-like hands and she slid down his body length easily in her silken robe, only stopping at his waist, where she wrapped her legs around him firmly. Her bottom was perched on his belt, so she asked him to remove it as it was digging into to her posterior.

"I'm not wearing a belt, ma'am," he said, looking into her eyes.

"Oh…" she sighed, "FUCKING TAKE ME NOW!"

His Lordship had eaten his supper, without choking on the pickled onions, and rang the bell.

"That'll be for you, Jack," said Mrs Spanner.

"That'll be for Phokker," he replied.

"E's busy with Kitty and Her Ladyship," she said, "So I suggest you shift yer arse upstairs!" Jack stood and made sure he was presentable, straightening his tie and waistcoat. He slowly walked upstairs and knocked gently on His Lordship's study door.

"Enter," came the reply. Jack walked in nervously and was wondering how Phokker would handle this.

"Can I help, sir?" he asked.

"Where's Phokker?" asked His Lordship, slightly put out.

"I'm afraid he has other business to attend to, sir," answered Jack, "but can I help at all?"

"I've finished my supper and I'd like to retire now," said His Lordship.

"I'll take your plate to the kitchen, sir," Jack said.

"Oh, leave that til after you've undressed me," huffed Lord Dickie. Jack had never undressed another man before and felt very uneasy about the whole thing. "Come on then!" quipped His Lordship, leading the way. Jack followed His Lordship to his room where he just stood and stared.

"You'll have to guide me, sir," said Jack, "I've never done this before."

"What, never?" said His Lordship, surprised.

"Never," squeaked Jack. Lord Dickie told Jack what to remove, how to fold it or where it was to hang carefully. His Lordship now stood before Jack with just his shorts, socks and gators on, his rounded tummy all plump like a Christmas pudding (only nowhere near as tasty and definitely **not** containing a sixpence!).

"Remove me gators carefully," said His Lordship, "The elastic snaps a bit vicious sometimes!" Jack removed them carefully, with no whiplash injuries for either of them, then removed his socks.

"Would you like your dressing gown on, sir?" asked Jack.

"Not really," answered Lord Dickie.

"Just the shorts to go." Jack gulped. He went to pull them down while he stood in front of him, but thought twice as he knew what he'd see before him. He stood behind His Lordship and pinched the merest bit of material between his forefinger and thumb and pulled down slowly. Jack turned away as he really didn't want to see Lord Dickie's wrinkly bum crack, but also knew of his fate if he was in front! His Lordship stepped out of his shorts and stood with his arms raised.

"Now what, sir?" Jack asked.

"My nightshirt, old chap," replied His Lordship.

"Where is it?" questioned Jack. His Lordship wobbled over to his tallboy and opened one of the drawers, removing a crisp, white nightshirt. He wobbled back over to Jack. Jack gawped at Lord Dickie's knob.

"Oh, this, dear boy," scoffed His Lordship, removing a bowtie from his flaccid wanger. "It's purely a comfort thing."

Chapter Fourteen

Phokker was just about to glide effortlessly into Her Ladyship's moist, silken purse, when they heard distant voices on the stairs. She leapt off of him and thrust him into the large wardrobe. She placed herself at her dressing table, combing through her hair once more. The voices trailed off so she went to see who had passed through the corridor. Her husband and Jack were going to His Lordship's room. She looked at the clock. Half past ten. "Early?" she mumbled to herself. But he'd had such an unpleasant encounter with Sir Sidney that he must have felt exhausted. She closed the door and locked it. She opened the wardrobe door and before she could give the all clear, Phokker yanked her inside. She ripped open her dressing gown to reveal…bugger all, actually, as it was so dark in there. As their eyes became accustomed to the very dim light, a long slither of light beamed through the empty keyhole, and Phokker could just make out the shape of her luscious, ripe breasts. He grabbed at them with his huge, hairy hands and squeezed them roughly. She moaned loudly.

"Sshhh," he whispered, "someone will hear you."

"In here?" she giggled. He pulled her closer and breathed in deeply.

"A bit fishy," he said.

"That'll be the kippers, not me!" she giggled again. The stench didn't put the pair off at all. She could feel his truncheon brushing against her tummy through his trousers and she wanted it released. She fumbled for his trouser buttons, but was taking ages. At this rate, he'd decorate his shorts like Jack!

"Let me do it," he said and he quickly undid them all. She reached in and grabbed his love stick.

"I want it in me now!" she exclaimed. He picked her up (this wardrobe is fucking massive by the way!) and wrapped her slender legs around his waist. "I do believe we were almost here before we were rudely interrupted," she said softly.

"I think I'm well overdue a birthday bang," he said.

"But it's not my birthday?" she said, bemused.

"But it is mine!" he declared.

"I had no idea!" she said, "I'd have bought you a gift."

"I'm getting the best present I've had in a long time!" he growled. She grabbed his neck tightly and waited with bated breath. He lowered her gently and with one hefty thrust, he slipped into her warm, wet bearded oyster. As she bounced up and down on his mutton dagger, the wardrobe swayed to and fro. He gripped her peachy buttocks tightly and the wardrobe swayed more and more. It rocked wildly as their thrusting intensified. Suddenly, and with enormous rapture, Phokker exploded and she screamed loudly. The wardrobe slammed to the floor with a shuddering thud. They were trapped. Phokker acted swiftly and kicked out at the back of the wardrobe until his huge size 12 shoes broke through. He heaved Her Ladyship out and stood the wardrobe upright. She ran into her bathroom and he told her to lock the door. His Lordship banged on Her Ladyship's door until Phokker opened it.

"What on earth is going on in here?" Lord Dickie cried.

"We had an intruder, sir," replied Phokker, with cobra-like reflexes.

"But you're all sweaty…and your shirt's torn," said Jack, who had followed His Lordship.

"I had to fight him off, sir," explained Phokker, wishing Jack would just fuck off.

"Where's my wife?" His Lordship asked, "Is she…is she…?"

"She's all right, sir," said Phokker, "I told her to lock herself in the bathroom for safety."

"Where's the bounder now?" Lord Dickie asked.

"He escaped out of the window, sir," replied Phokker, "He must have seen the open windows and thought he'd struck gold, sir."

"But how…?" Jack was just about to ask how the intruder had climbed up the wall in the first place, but Phokker anticipated this and shut Jack down quickly by telling him to fetch Kitty immediately to assist Her Ladyship. He left straight away.

"It was a good job you were close by, old boy," said His Lordship, who tapped at his wife's bathroom door.

"Are you all right, my dear?" he asked tenderly. Her heart was racing and for a few seconds she couldn't find the words to answer him.

"Just…just…a bit shocked, my dearest," she replied, all sickly sweet.

"As long as you're definitely all right," he said, "Kitty will be here soon." Her Ladyship put on her bathrobe and tied it tightly around her waist. It was warm and comforting. She stepped out into her bedroom looking slightly dazed, confused and bedraggled.

"Dear Lord!" His Lordship exclaimed, "What did the bastard do to you?"

"Nothing, my dear," she replied.

"But you look positively ravished!" he scoffed.

"The intruder never laid a finger on me," she said, looking at Phokker, while her husband gave her a hug.

"Close the windows, Phokker, and make sure they're locked securely!" he demanded.

"Yes, sir," replied Phokker and he did as he was asked, "No one will get in here now, sir."

"Thank you for caring, darling," she purred.

"Oh, that's all right, my dear," Lord Dickie said, giving her another tight squeeze. But that sentiment was not for her husband.

Jack was still puzzled at how anyone could have climbed up that wall and entered Her Ladyship's room. "Her Ladyship wants you, Kitty," said Jack as he walked into the kitchen.

"She's in the wash house, steaming Her Ladyship's things," said Mrs Spanner. Jack went out into the cold night air and darted into the wash house. Steam was everywhere and he couldn't see.

"Shut the bloody door!" shouted Kitty, "The steam's getting away!"

"Her Ladyship wants you," he said, closing the door.

"Oh, it's you, Jack," said Kitty, "What does she want now?"

"There's been another intruder," he said, "This time in Her Ladyship's room."

"Well bugger me!" exclaimed Kitty. All this time the steam encompassed them and they couldn't see each other.

"Why all the steam?" asked Jack.

"Best way I can fink of getting rid of the stink from Her Ladyship's fings," replied Kitty, "Give us an 'and to 'ang um up in the kitchen." Jack opened the door and the steam escaped into the chilly night air. It made Kitty's nipples stand out like accordion buttons. Jack just stared. "You like what you see?" she asked him. Jack had no words but his mind raced, his groin began to ache and he was finding it extremely difficult to think of anything to distract himself. He closed his eyes and started to breathe deeply and slowly. All he could see was her 'nibbles' (as his mother called them) pointing at him.

"This is getting really hard!" Jack yelped helplessly, trying to think of any kind of distraction.

"Is it?" asked Kitty, looking at his groin, "Oh yeah, I sees what you mean!" Jack covered himself with his hands and walked backwards. "Oh no you don't!" said Kitty, "You can 'elp carry this lot!" Jack bent forward, trying to hide his embarrassment, and took some gowns from Kitty. "Don't be so bloody daft, Jack," she said, "And don't be trying to hide it neiver. I seen too many of them (so Queenie says) and I bet yours is no bloody different from any of um!" Jack flushed a hot pink; luckily it was dark. "Don't be embarrassed," she said, "I loves ya."

"You...you...love me?" he asked.

"Course I does!" she smiled and she flung her arms around his neck and kissed him.

"Have I got any clean shorts left?" he asked. Fuck me, not AGAIN?!

Phokker and His Lordship left Her Ladyship and wandered off to His Lordship's room.

"Do you think she'll be all right, old chap?" asked Lord Dickie.

"After a good night's rest, I'm sure she'll be fine, sir," answered Phokker.

"Do you think I should have stayed with her?" Lord Dickie asked, still quite concerned about his wife.

"As I said, sir, a good night's rest is all she needs," Phokker replied.

"Mmm, she can probably do so without me lusting after her…after what she's just been through," said His Lordship.

"Exactly, sir," said Phokker.

"Well, I'll keep an ear out for any nonsense," quipped Lord Dickie, "And I'll be in there like a shot!"

"I'd do exactly the same if I were you, sir," replied Phokker as he turned down His Lordship's bed. "I'm afraid there's no bed warmer," Phokker said apologetically, "what with all the fuss earlier."

"No matter, dear boy, just throw on an extra blanket and I'll be fine," said His Lordship. Phokker plumped the pillows and tucked His Lordship in super-tight. He placed an extra blanket over the end of the bed and wished His Lordship a restful night's sleep. He was hoping he was going to be out for the count all night, as he wanted more wardrobe shenanigans…without the wardrobe this time!

Kitty knocked and then entered Her Ladyship's room, but she wasn't there. She turned to leave with a 'For fuck sake' under her breath when Her Ladyship came out from her bathroom.

"Ah there you are, Kitty," said Her Ladyship, "Can you help me retire for the night, I'm exhausted." Kitty turned down Her Ladyship's bed and noticed that she too, had no bed warmer.

"I'll fetch you up one in a mo," said Kitty.

"Thank you, so kind," replied Her Ladyship (getting on like a house on fire these two! I hope they can keep this shit up?). Her Ladyship sat at her dressing table and fingered through her hair wistfully.

"You must be ever so shaken, ma'am," said Kitty, "What wif annuver intruder."

"How did you know?" she asked.

"Jack told me," answered Kitty, "I bet he was a brute!"

"Oh, er, yes, yes indeed, awful man," Her Ladyship lied. She was pretty crap at lying. Nowhere near as quick or as inventive as Phokker. "Yes, he was huge with a straggly, ginger beard and...and...he only had one eye," said Her Ladyship.

"I hope 'e dint hurt you?" Kitty enquired.

"Phokker was here luckily," she answered, "So I was well looked after." (that's for sure!)

"Where would we all be wivout 'im, eh?" Kitty sighed, holding out Her Ladyship's nightgown. She dressed her quickly and helped her to bed.

"I'll be right back wiv the bed warmer," said Kitty, "So don't lock the door just yet. Her Ladyship snuggled down and closed her eyes. Kitty met Phokker on the landing.

"She's very calm for a bird who's nearly been got at!" exclaimed Kitty. "Did you see 'im? The intruder?"

"Yes, not much of a fellow, so I easily overpowered him," lied Phokker, lightning fast. "No match for me."

"So, he wasn't huge then?" Kitty asked.

"No, no, not huge," answered Phokker, "Plain looking really; a bit scruffy and dirty. Probably a tramp trying his luck."

"So, he dint have a ginger beard?" Kitty quizzed again.

"No, no beard," replied Phokker.

"What colour was his eyes?" she asked.

"Blue, I think, but I can't be too sure," he lied again.

"What? Both of um?" she asked, confused by now.

"Er, yes, both of them," he answered, "But what's with all the questions?"

"Oh, er, Jack just said annuver intruder, dint give no say in what he looked like," said Kitty.

"I'm getting her bed warmer now."

"I'll see if she requires any hot drinks, or a night cap," said Phokker.

"Shall I wait 'ere so I can fetch um too?" she asked.

"No need," he snapped, "Take your time."

Kitty wandered back to the kitchen, quite puzzled at their different descriptions, and felt confused by it all.

Chapter Fifteen

Phokker tapped lightly on Her Ladyship's door and walked in without a word. "That was quick, Kitty," said Her Ladyship, with her eyes still closed. Phokker didn't reply, but quietly stepped towards her bed and sat down, placing a hand on her thigh. "Kitty!" Her Ladyship exclaimed, sitting upright. "Oh…"

She opened her eyes and then flung her arms around his neck. "Is it so wrong, what we're doing?"

"I've no doubt it is, but I can't stop," replied Phokker.

"You're like a drug. Addictive," she said.

"We could both be ruined if this ever got out," he whispered, breathing heavily in her ear.

"But I doubt anyone suspects a thing," she said.

"Mrs Spanner does," he replied, "and Kitty was asking silly questions out on the landing just now."

"What about?" she asked.

"If the intruder had a ginger beard," he replied, "And what colour his eyes were." She looked at him nervously and told him of the description she'd given Kitty. He told her what he'd said. Totally different. "Kitty won't think twice of it, so don't worry," he said, rubbing her shoulders.

"Don't start anything, she'll be back soon," said Her Ladyship. "I've left something for you in my laundry basket," she whispered. Phokker went into her bathroom (something he very rarely did…or any man for that matter, not even her husband!) and in the basket was her crisp, white bloomers, with the pink rosebuds on the cheeks. "Keep them under your pillow," she told him. He tucked them into his waistcoat as best as he could.

"Thank you very much," he smiled. More wanking off material!

"You best tuck me in again," she said, "She'll be back soon." She lay down and she was tightly tucked in. He leaned over and gently kissed her forehead. She closed her eyes and gave a most comforting sigh. As he opened the door, Kitty was stood with the bed warmer. She looked at him and smiled, but didn't say anything. She announced herself to Her Ladyship, who pulled her feet up out of the way so Kitty could place the bed warmer near her feet.

"It ain't too 'ot, ma'am," Kitty said, "so your toes will be cosy soon enough."

"Thank you, Kitty," said Her Ladyship, without opening her eyes once. Kitty waltzed past Phokker without a word, but stood waiting at the top of the stairs.

"Goodnight, ma'am," he said dutifully and closed the door.

"Mrs Spanner's got a nice cup 'o' cocoa waiting fer you," Kitty said. He heard Her Ladyship lock her door. Damn it! No early morning, sneaking out of bed, fumblings for him!

When Phokker walked into the kitchen, Jack was well relaxed, sipping his cocoa. Kitty sat down in the chair next to him and Mrs Spanner was at the range beginning a new batch of gravy. (Heaven help us!) Phokker could hear her mumbling to herself, wittering some witch-like, ancient incantation to brew up her latest batch. He was waiting for a puff of green smog to appear about her when he sat and took a sip of his cocoa. He spat it right back in his cup. "This tastes awful!" he declared.

"It's what liars deserve!" Mrs Spanner bit back. Kitty looked nervously at Jack, who as always was absolutely clueless.

"I wanna word with you," Mrs Spanner snarled, "Courtyard, now!" She stormed out of the kitchen door and stood in the yard, arms firmly crossed, tapping her foot loudly. Kitty looked at Phokker and he knew that she must have mentioned something to Mrs Spanner. He threw his cocoa into the sink, smashing the cup, went calmly into the courtyard, closing the kitchen door behind him. "You bloody liar!" she yelled.

"Will you keep your voice down! You'll wake them!" he hissed, pointing upwards.

"You an 'er are startin' somefin, I knows it now!" she hissed back. He pushed her into the washroom and closed the door. Kitty's face was pressed against the kitchen window, as she knelt on the draining board but she couldn't see them let alone hear then now.

"What are you on about?" he asked her, full of fury.

"You said the intruder was small wiv blue eyes," she fumed, "An 'Er said he 'ad a ginger beard and one eye!" Phokker just stared at her, with his arms across his taut chest. His heart was racing but he showed no trace, nor hint of worry on his face. "Can't even get your stories straight!" she huffed.

"For your information, Her Ladyship didn't see the intruder as I had made her lock herself in her bathroom. My description is accurate. Just look what he did to my shirt!" Phokker said most agitated, grabbing at his torn shirt.

"She coulda done that!" she barked, again with her arms crossed firmly across her hefty bosoms.

"She couldn't harm a fly, let alone rip a shirt!" he scoffed.

"Anyfink is possible in fits of passion!" she bellowed.

"Do you honestly think she would lower herself to do such a thing?" he asked.

"Like I said, anyfinks possible," she said. He lowered his arms, palms facing forward.

"Do you honestly think I would jeopardise my position within this household for a quick fumble?" he asked her, "After all His Lordship has done for me!"

Mrs Spanner suddenly felt a pang of guilt as she listened to those words, the way he'd uttered them with integrity and the utmost sincerity. "So why she say what she said?" she asked.

"I'm guessing that shock set in and she had a picture of a villainous looking character in her mind," he answered, rather convincingly.

"And I thought..." she started.

"And you thought wrong," he finished. He opened the door for her and politely gave a nod for her to walk out first. They returned to the kitchen, where she set about making a fresh cup of cocoa for him. Mrs Spanner took Kitty into the larder and told her what Phokker had said. She was still a little confused but was pleased that Phokker had told the truth. Little did they know! They sat chatting while Phokker went about the house, locking all the downstairs doors and windows, making sure all was secure for the night. When he returned, Mrs Spanner told him to leave his torn shirt in the laundry, as she'd have a go at trying to mend it. She was a dab hand at fixing anything. She even shod a horse once, but that's another story! They each had their tiny lamps to light their way up the back stairs and in turn, went to their rooms.

"Remember to lock your doors everyone...sleep well," said Phokker and he watched each of them retire to their rooms and lock themselves in. He locked his door and started to undress. Her Ladyship's bloomers fell to the floor and he swiftly scooped them up, giving them a great, big sniff. He grinned widely and placed them under his pillow. Putting his shirt on the back of the chair, he was annoyed that it was ripped, but not by how it had occurred. Mrs Spanner would fix it beautifully. He climbed into his cold bed but the warmth he felt inside meant that he didn't much care. The moonlight chinked its way through a gap in the curtains. His eyes followed its beam so far across the room, until they became heavy. He'd save the bloomers to crack one off another time; he fell asleep in no time at all.

Jack was woken by loud crashing and thudding and knew exactly where it was coming from. Phokker was shouting. "MOLLY! MOLLY!" and his voice grew louder and louder. Jack ran out into the hallway to find Mrs Spanner and Kitty there too.

"I'll sort him out, I did last night!" said Jack. He banged on the door and tried to get in, but it was locked tight. Mrs Spanner ran off, but returned quickly, with a bit of old newspaper and a knitting needle. "This isn't the time for knitting!" Jack squawked.

"Move out me way!" she said, shoving him to one side. She placed the newspaper under the door and poked the knitting needle into the keyhole. They heard the key drop to the floor and she pulled the newspaper towards her. She picked up the key and handed it to Jack.

"That was brilliant, Mrs S!" he said.

"I'll remember that!" said Kitty, winking at Jack, who really didn't have a clue why she'd want Phokker's key. (Twat!) Jack unlocked the door and they all gawped inside. His room was totally trashed and he was writhing on the floor with his limbs having the most awful spasms. Mrs Spanner picked up a jug from his chest of drawers and threw the remaining contents onto his face. His eyes became wide.

"WHAT THE FUCK!" he bellowed. This startled them as they'd never, ever heard him use such language before.

"You've trashed your room," said Jack. Phokker sat up and looked about him. With their tiny lamps lighting his room, he could see that they were indeed, correct. He stood and started to pick things up, but became unsteady and fell to his knees. Jack helped him up. "You can come and sleep in my room," Jack said. "Kitty, Mrs S, can you move his mattress to my room please?" They did as he asked and brought in his blankets too. Jack steadied Phokker as they walked to Jack's room. "You can have my bed," said Jack, helping him sit down. "I'll sleep on the floor."

"Thank you," said Phokker softly, feeling ashamed and embarrassed. Phokker suddenly remembered his newly acquired wanking material and insisted on going back to tidy his room.

"We'll do it in the morning," said Jack, "It's too dark now."

"Goodnight," said Mrs Spanner and Kitty in unison, and returned to their rooms. Phokker heaved a sigh of relief. They couldn't have seen the bloomers in the dimly lit room...wherever they ended up? Jack placed the blankets on the mattress laid on the floor.

"You get some rest, Phokker," said Jack.

"Can I have a drink of water please?" asked Phokker.

"The carafe's on the side," Jack replied. Phokker went to pour himself a glass of water. As he did so, something shimmery moved in the glass. He placed the glass back down on the side and stepped back. He picked up the tiny lamp and nervously walked back towards the side. Waving the lamp to and fro, he caught a glimpse of golden flashes flittering about the glass. "Oh, I forgot about that," said Jack, "Sorry." Phokker just stood and stared with his eyes on stalks, mouth emulating the very thing that was in the glass. "That's my prize from the fair," said Jack, "I didn't have anywhere else to put it, so I popped it in there."

"Go...go...gold...f...fi...fish..." stuttered Phokker.

"Is there anything wrong?" asked Jack.

"MOLLY!" cried Phokker.